She couldn't escape — this fascination...

Desperate, Natalie tried to struggle free of the demanding arms that held her tightly. This man would pretend anything—even that he loved her—to get what he wanted.

Abruptly he let her go. His eyes gleamed. "So, you despise me, do you?" he teased. But he didn't hear her muffled reply as she tore past him.

Why had she agreed to accompany him, alone, to the seashore—a man she knew was a criminal, a blackmailer?

Other

MYSTIQUE BOOKS

by MARIANNE ANDRAU

For a free catalogue listing all available Mystique Books,
send your name and address to:

MYSTIQUE BOOKS
1440 South Priest Drive, Tempe, AZ 85281
In Canada: 649 Ontario St., Stratford, Ontario N5A 6W2

Mask of Destiny

by MARIANNE ANDRAU

MYSTIQUE BOOKS
TORONTO • LONDON • NEW YORK
HAMBURG • AMSTERDAM • STOCKHOLM

MASK OF DESTINY / first published December 1981

ISBN 0-373-50155-2

PRINTED IN CANADA

Chapter 1

Impatiently Natalie Davis brushed back a strand of long black hair that had strayed over her cheek. Unaccustomed to the air conditioning, she felt hot and cold at the same time and wondered idly if she was coming down with something.

As she walked down the long wide corridor of the second floor of Monte Carlo's famous Hotel de Paris, she reflected, for the umpteenth time that day, if she really were cut out to be a maid, even for only three months. She didn't seem to be able to get used to the hotel, with its opulent prewar sophistication and almost nineteenth-century elegance. Often she felt intimidated and was constantly afraid of doing the wrong thing in front of all these rich and haughty people.

But it was only her second week, Natalie reminded herself. And, once the day was over, her time was her own. She could swim in any one of the hotel pools or go to the public beach, and there were always plenty of things to see and people to watch—even if a girl didn't have enough money to spend at Monte Carlo's fabulous casinos.

Alone in the privacy of her room, as she fixed her hair Natalie considered whether she should have it cut short. Then she could just wash it and shake it dry, for it would curl naturally.

She knew, however, that she was just playing with the idea out of boredom, for twisted on top of her head and laced through an old hair comb that had once been her mother's, her glossy black hair was one of her most beautiful features. Two tendrils curled delicately at each cheek, emphasizing her high cheekbones and her large, beautifully shaped liquid green eyes with their long thick eyelashes.

Later, as she paused for a moment to straighten her skirt, Natalie glanced at her reflection in the glass paneling of the corridor walls.

"Not bad for a linen maid," she murmured to herself for confidence and knocked briskly on the door of Room 215.

Taken aback by the sudden pounding of her heart, Natalie wasn't sure if anyone had heard her and she knocked again.

"Come in. The door's open."

The light girlish voice surprised Natalie. So far, all the female hotel guests she'd met had been older . . . as well as, of course, the businessmen. The women had been haughty and incredibly well dressed. The men had been self-confident and, Natalie reminded herself wryly, not above giving her a second glance as long as their wives or girl friends were looking the other way.

Abruptly she remembered the night of her arrival in Monaco. It had been the last time that a man who was not a guest at the hotel had seemed to take an interest in her. Excited and unable to sleep, she had decided to take a stroll down to the harbor. Dressed only in a light summer shift and sandals, her trench coat over her arm, she had wandered along the pier, feeling its gentle rise and fall as the yachts bumped against their moorings. Thinking she was alone, Natalie had indulged in a little fantasy in which, instead of a poor English student, she was a member of the European jet set, interested in buying one of the yachts in the harbor. To her surprise they had begun to look quite different. Some of them were actually quite shabby. Natalie had had to smile at herself. Obviously she would have no trouble adapting to wealth, to the luxury of being able to demand the best in everything. Not that there was much chance, she reminded herself glumly. Being a linen maid in Monte Carlo was probably as close as she'd ever come to consorting with the wealthy.

Suddenly Natalie's privacy had been shattered by a cough. Startled and a little uneasy, she'd looked quickly around. Standing a few feet away from her was a sailor— or at least that's what she'd assumed him to be, for he was dressed in white pants and a red-and-white T-shirt that showed off his powerfully muscled arms and rich tan. He wore a sailor's cap on top of a head of thick, black curly hair. He flicked his cigarette into the water and smiled.

"It's late for a young lady to be out. No?"

"Yes," Natalie began nervously. "I mean, no, not really. You see . . . ." She stopped, annoyed with herself. Why was she explaining herself to this man? It was none of his business. "I've just arrived," she said icily. "I thought I would take a walk before going to bed."

Natalie almost choked as a scream rose in her throat.

The sailor was reaching into his pocket for . . . a knife? Frightened, she watched as he walked slowly toward her, holding something in his hand.

"Would you like some? A toast to your visit to Monte Carlo?"

She saw that he was holding a bottle and almost fainted with relief. Flooded with embarrassment, Natalie hoped her voice would not give her away. She would die if he had guessed what she was thinking.

"What is it?"

The sailor grinned. "Absinthe."

Natalie hesitated. Although she had lived in Paris for three years, she had never tasted this famous drink. But as she was about to refuse, she remembered why she had come to Monte Carlo in the first place and said, as firmly as she could, "Thanks. I'd love some."

The sailor introduced himself as Fernando Rodriquez. He was from the Basque region of Spain, he explained, and spent his summers and winters working up and down the French or Spanish rivieras. As they strolled toward the hotel, Fernando pointed out to her the yacht on which he worked. It seemed enormous to Natalie, much to Fernando's amusement. Laughingly he reassured her that, in comparison with some of the yachts that docked regularly at Monte Carlo, it was very ordinary indeed.

When they'd said goodbye the attractive Spaniard had kissed Natalie's hand with a flourish and promised to take her dancing the next time he was in Monte Carlo.

That night, as she got ready for bed in her tiny maid's quarters, Natalie had reflected happily that she had been right, after all, to come to Monte Carlo. Less than ten hours after her arrival she had already met a tall handsome man. It was a pleasant change from the monotonous student life she had been leading in Paris, and she felt she deserved it.

But Fernando hadn't contacted her again.

It was proving more difficult than she had thought it would be to meet people, Natalie reflected now as she took the passkey from the pocket in her skirt. She let herself into Room 215 and quietly closed the door behind her. She'd stepped into one of the most luxurious suites in the hotel and the entrance hall alone was larger than most hotel rooms she had seen. The dark oak floor echoed with the sound of her light footsteps as she crossed into the living room.

Natalie knew that the suite was occupied by one Señorita Ramona Martinez, the daughter of the well-known Spanish millionaire-coffee magnate, Arturo Martinez. Although Martinez was not an ostentatious person, his daughter certainly was. In spite of her Catholic upbringing, Ramona burned the candles at both ends, or so the other maids, always eager to gossip, had told Natalie when she'd mentioned she would be standing in for the chambermaid who usually looked after Room 215.

The large living room was carpeted in white and furnished with delicate, exquisitely carved Chinese wood-and-bamboo furniture. It looked clean and unused. Only one corner marred the perfect ordered elegance of the room, where it was crowded with carelessly thrown leather luggage. Miss Martinez obviously was sure there was plenty more where that came from, Natalie thought ruefully. She, on the other hand, would have had to give a month's pay for a set of luggage like that—that is, if she didn't need the money more for her next year's tuition.

But Natalie forgot all about the luggage when she viewed the famous harbor. Working inside all day, she sometimes forgot that just outside these four walls there was a brilliant blue sky, silver skyscrapers glistening in the sun and clusters of boats bumping companionably against one another in the harbor.

Suddenly a voluptuous young woman, clad only in a long white negligee with an enormous red flower across the front, drew back the sliding doors and crossed over from the balcony into the suite. Ramona Martinez must have been admiring the magnificent view, as well. When she noticed Natalie standing near the hallway she pointed to a silver tray with the remnants of a light breakfast scattered on it. "The tray is over there," she said abruptly. "I rang for it to be taken away fifteen minutes ago."

Natalie, however, was too surprised by Ramona Martinez's appearance to do anything except stare rather openly at her. It was not Ramona's beauty that shocked her, although the woman was, with her thick black hair, high cheekbones and regal air, decidedly stunning. It was the amazing similarity in their appearance. Natalie felt as if she were looking at her double. Ramona was not as slim nor her features as delicate as Natalie's but the resemblance was distinct and unmistakable. Ramona, though, seemed oblivious. Seeing that Natalie had made no move to pick up the tray, she repeated her instructions.

"I beg your pardon, madam," Natalie murmured. This was the first time since she'd begun work at the hotel that anyone had spoken to her in such dismissive tones, and she wasn't sure she had the self-control to submit without a protest to such treatment.

For a moment the beautiful Spanish woman frowned,

then she looked more closely at Natalie. Her frown disappeared and she said quickly, in a completely different tone of voice, "Oh, I do beg your pardon! I rang for someone to come take away my tray." She pointed to the tray again. "Who are you?"

"I'm the hotel linen maid, madam. Your regular chambermaid, Katrina, has her day off today and she asked me to pick up a dress that you wanted pressed for this evening."

Ramona was all smiles now. "Ah, of course. Now I understand."

As the woman walked to the closet that stretched the entire length of one wall and began searching for the dress, Natalie examined her unreservedly. She certainly was a beautiful woman. Full figured and graceful, her almond-shaped eyes, slender neck and long dark hair gave her an exotic air. Like many women of her country, she had evidently matured early.

Ramona let out a sigh of annoyance. "I'm sure that the dress is in here somewhere! I can never find anything I want in here. There just isn't enough room."

Suddenly the ring of the telephone startled them both. Ramona jumped and Natalie turned to leave, sure that Ramona would want her to wait in the foyer until the conversation was over. But Ramona stopped her with an imperious gesture.

"It's not necessary for you to leave. I'll only be a moment."

It was obvious to Natalie that she was used to being obeyed, but although she disliked the Spanish girl's manner Natalie couldn't help studying her as she picked up the telephone receiver. Ramona Martinez had given no sign that she'd noticed the resemblance between herself and the linen maid. And probably that was why, Natalie decided. The last thing Ramona would want to recognize would be that she and a mere linen maid could have anything in common.

To Natalie's surprise, Ramona's expression changed abruptly as she lifted the receiver. All her haughtiness disappeared and she suddenly seemed far more unsure of herself.

"Oh, it's you again." Ramona spoke softly, so that Natalie could barely hear her. "I might have known."

As Ramona listened to her caller, it was clear to Natalie that she was trying, but not succeeding, to put on a brave front. Something was upsetting her a great deal. Her lips quivered and there was an uncertainty in her voice that the caller couldn't fail to hear. Ramona must have heard it, too, for she made an effort to sound more authoritative.

"Of course, I'm still waiting! I would have called you earlier if there was any news. I'm trying to get in touch with him. Yes, yes . . . of course, I'll call you as soon as I hear."

The lost, childlike expression on Ramona's face went straight to Natalie's heart. As she hung up the receiver, Ramona shivered and looked as though she was about to burst into tears.

"I'm cold," she whispered.

Natalie walked quickly to the doors leading to the balcony, to make sure they were firmly closed. The noise seemed to remind Ramona of her presence.

"Oh, I'm sorry. I was trying to find a dress for you to iron, wasn't I?"

But once again Ramona seemed unable to shake herself out of her troubled mood. She stood gazing at the crowded closet, deep in thought. She seemed so genuinely troubled that Natalie almost felt sorry for her. She was so lovely, probably the toast of Monte Carlo . . . it was hard to believe she could really be unhappy.

Not wanting to embarrass Ramona by staring at her, but increasingly curious about what was disturbing her, Natalie began to examine the room more carefully. Her eyes fell on a large black-and-white photograph set in a silver frame. It was of Ramona, the shot lighted so as to emphasize her high cheekbones and her sultry smile. Looking at the photograph, then at the troubled girl lost in thought in front of her, Natalie could hardly believe that this was the same person. What could possibly be wrong, she wondered. Surely Ramona Martinez had everything in the world anyone could ever ask for? Money, clothes, beauty, youth and friends . . . .

Ramona, who had reluctantly begun looking through her closet, now turned to Natalie. She held up an exquisite dress of orange chiffon, covered with a delicate leaflike pattern that was obviously hand-sewn. Natalie was sure it was a designer's original. Perhaps it had even been made especially for Ramona, she thought, the soft material and the cut complementing her so perfectly.

"I've only been here three weeks and already everything is crushed," Ramona complained. If the woman could be irritated by such a trivial matter, Natalie decided, relieved, there probably wasn't much the matter with her.

Ramona looked at Natalie sharply. "Are you the girl who ironed my dress the other day?"

Evidently Ramona was back in form, but Natalie managed to hold her tongue. She certainly didn't envy Katrina her job!

"No, madam. Until yesterday, we had two linen maids. But the girl who did your dress last time left for her holidays, and I'm in charge of all the ironing until she comes back."

"Are you sure . . ." Ramona began, obviously hesitating, but unwilling to stop. "You can see that this dress is very delicate. . . . I'm so concerned that it be ironed carefully. It's very important that I look perfect tonight."

Natalie had to admit that Ramona was right: it would be very difficult to iron the dress well. The material was so delicate that the slightest miscalculation in the temperature of the iron might scorch it.

"I'll do my very best, madam," Natalie replied in what she hoped was a reassuring tone of voice.

The dress now folded carefully over her arm, Natalie turned to leave but Ramona stopped her with another question.

"What is your name?"

"Natalie Davis," she answered.

Natalie expected that, her curiosity satisfied, Ramona would let her leave. But no, the mysterious phone call and its troublesome aftereffects seemingly forgotten, Ramona had now decided to turn all her attention to Natalie. Could she be lonely, Natalie wondered. Again the thought crossed her mind that perhaps Ramona Martinez's life wasn't all that it appeared to be.

Ramona smiled. "You must forgive me, Miss Davis. It's just that . . . well, you see, you don't look like a linen maid. That's all. For one thing, you're so young. If I had seen you anywhere else, I would have thought you were a student."

Natalie said nothing.

Thinking that she had offended this slender hotel employee with her quiet yet elegant manner, Ramona rushed on. "Oh, please don't misunderstand!" she said. "There's nothing whatever the matter with being a linen maid. I'm sure that it's demanding work. It's just that . . . ."

And Ramona stopped, confused. Suddenly she seemed very young and awkward. Natalie, realizing that she was just trying to be friendly, decided to tell her what she wanted to know.

"You're not all that wrong about me, madam. I *am* a student. From Paris. I'm working here as a linen maid. It's just a summer job, though, and in September I'll be returning to Paris."

"But you're not French?"

"Oh, no. I'm from England. But I've been studying at the Sorbonne for three years now."

"The Sorbonne!" Ramona exclaimed. In her excitement she looked even more like a schoolgirl than an international heiress. "I was a student there as well!"

Natalie found her natural reserve melting under the influence of Ramona's enthusiasm. She listened with a smile as Ramona babbled on in French. "I'm really proud of myself for having been right about you. I'm still studying, you know. At Madrid. I'm taking French."

"You speak the language very well," Natalie said reassuringly.

"Well, perhaps." Ramona seemed doubtful. "I've got a

pretty good vocabulary but my accent is terrible. I don't think I'll ever get the French 'r.' It's so different from the Spanish one."

Natalie laughed in agreement. "Oh, I know. I have the same trouble with the Spanish 'r' that you have with the French one."

"You speak Spanish?" Ramona asked eagerly.

"Oh, yes," Natalie answered in Spanish. "I'm studying French, Spanish and Russian at the Sorbonne. I want to work in the diplomatic service after I get my degree."

Natalie was pleased to see that Ramona was impressed.

"The diplomatic service," she mused, now in English. "But wouldn't you be frightened? Nowadays there is so much violence, so much terrorism. . . . Diplomats, it seems, are always being kidnapped and held for ransom."

Natalie smiled. "That's not really true, you know. When you think of all the diplomats there are in the world, only a small percentage of them ever get kidnapped. Their job is no more dangerous than an airplane pilot's. Probably less so. And besides, I want some adventure in my life. It's been too—"

Natalie suddenly checked herself. She had been on the verge of telling a total stranger about her most private feelings, something that shocked her. Ramona Martinez was a guest who, on a mere whim, could have her sent packing from the Hotel de Paris. In a rush, Natalie realized how lonely she must be, to have almost confided in a stranger. And, Natalie promised herself, she would have to watch herself. Ramona might ask her questions that, out of politeness and concern for her job, she would feel obliged to answer.

Ramona, though, gave no indication that she'd noticed Natalie's withdrawal. She was clearly fascinated by the slim, dark-haired English girl with her air of self-contained dignity, and she kept on with her eager questions, not sensing, or refusing to pay attention to, Natalie's obvious desire to leave.

"What do you do when you aren't talking to me?" Ramona inquired mischievously.

"I work in a small room off the hotel laundry, ironing and mending."

"What a strange existence some people lead," Ramona commented, half to herself.

"Oh, don't go painting a bleak picture of my life, Miss Martinez," Natalie said quickly. "I have every evening off, as well as two full days a week to myself. I swim and play tennis, and even visit the casinos. It's great," she ended, sounding defensive even to her own ears.

"You visit the casinos?" Ramona looked closely at Natalie. "You like to gamble?"

"Well, not very much." Natalie was reluctant to admit that since she'd arrived in Monte Carlo she'd spent most of her evenings in her room curled up with a book.

But Ramona was paying no attention to what Natalie was saying. "I love the casinos! I love gambling," she declared.

Surprised by the tone of Ramona's voice, Natalie glanced sharply at her. There was an intensity, a tightness in her speech that had made Natalie instantly feel uncomfortable. For the first time since she had met her, Natalie thought that Ramona looked like what she was supposed to be—a sophisticated heiress.

"I don't think it's much fun to run the risk of losing all your money," Natalie said, hoping to change the subject and leave as soon as she could.

"Oh, but you don't always lose! I've won from time to time. I love it," Ramona went on a bit wildly, Natalie thought. "When I gamble I feel more alive. Life seems more exciting, more real. I feel as though I can remember those moments forever. How old do you think I am?" she asked abruptly.

"About twenty?" Natalie was somehow sure that Ramona was younger than this, in spite of her mature appearance.

"I'm twenty-one. That means I'm an adult in the eyes of the law."

"But what does that have to—"

Before Natalie could finish Ramona interrupted and went on compulsively, "It means that my father shouldn't treat me like a child! I have no money. The only way that I could convince him to let me stay in Monte Carlo was to promise him I wouldn't gamble. And he wouldn't even take my word! He paid my hotel bill in advance. Worse, he left instructions with the cashier that he was to dole me out a small sum of money every day—just enough to cover my most basic needs. In short, he's cut me right off." Ramona laughed bitterly.

Natalie wasn't sure if Ramona was exaggerating for effect. She was probably bored and eager to impress a mere linen maid with her tales of decadence, Natalie thought. She certainly hoped it was no more serious than that. Still, she couldn't resist replying to Ramona's comments.

"It sounds as though your father has good reason not to leave you with much money at your disposal."

Ramona suddenly grew anxious again and her face took on the same worried expression of a few minutes earlier. She seemed about to say something, then sighed and looked out through the window at the harbor. Its tranquillity and beauty seemed to be offering her a brief escape from her troubles.

Natalie was torn between her desire to leave and a growing warmth for this young Spanish heiress, who was so clearly spoiled and confused. She hoped that Ramona, who was obviously impulsive, wouldn't tell her more than she should.

Finally the urge to confess seemed to overwhelm Ramona's reserve and she turned toward Natalie, looking at her with an eager expression.

"The truth," she began in excited tones, "is that my father *did* know what he was doing! My gambling goes back a long way and he is all too painfully aware of it." Ramona paused, but as Natalie made no effort to comment, she continued, "I can't get along without a lot of money, even for someone of my position in life. I'm trying to change, Natalie, but it's hard. Why am I telling you all this? What an idiot I am!"

Eager to reassure her, Natalie said quickly, "You needed to talk to someone, madam. I happened to be here, that's all. I know how it is when you're lonely. Sometimes it's important to be able to talk to someone, and it's easier to speak openly with a stranger."

"But I didn't say anything about being lonely!"

"Well, perhaps I was wrong," Natalie continued calmly. "At any rate, please don't worry about anything you might have said. I can assure you that I would never betray the confidence of a guest of the hotel." Determined to leave, she smiled and said, "And now, if you don't mind, I'll just take this dress downstairs to be ironed."

The expression on Ramona's face changed. "Please excuse my strange behavior, Natalie," she apologized. "There's a lot on my mind these days. I know that you have work to do, but I just want to say that it's been a pleasure meeting you. I hope we'll have a chance to talk again."

Natalie doubted it. Still smiling, she turned, eager to leave the changeable Miss Martinez for the more predictable companionship of the other hotel maids and bellhops.

Suddenly the telephone rang again. Startled, Ramona turned a frightened gaze on Natalie. She made no move toward the telephone, which continued to ring. It was almost, Natalie mused, as if the caller sensed that Ramona was standing beside the telephone, unwilling to answer it.

"Madam, the telephone," she said patiently. What could this wealthy young woman possibly be afraid of?

"I know," came the reply. But Ramona didn't move. She reached out a pleading hand to Natalie. "Please, answer it for me. Ask who it is. If . . . if it's Carlos Vilar, tell him that I've gone out."

Not giving herself time to think, Natalie walked to the phone and picked up the receiver.

"Who's speaking?" she asked, glancing quickly at Ramona, who stood with a look of near terror in her eyes as she watched Natalie.

For Ramona's benefit, Natalie repeated slowly, and deliberately. "Mr. Carlos Vilar . . . Carlos Vilar. Yes, I've got that. No, Mr. Vilar, Miss Martinez isn't here at the moment. She just went out. I'm the . . . maid. Yes, I'll tell her you called." Silently she replaced the receiver.

"What did he say?" Ramona's face was ashen.

Natalie hesitated, unwilling to repeat the man's exact words.

"Tell me; I must know what he said!" Unaware of what she was doing, Ramona twisted her hands nervously.

"He said, 'Tell Miss Martinez I called. Tell her I'm sorry that I couldn't meet her, but I'll be seeing her soon enough. It won't do her any harm to wait. Tell her I'll be there at nine o'clock this evening, as arranged.' "

Ramona visibly relaxed at these words and her fear turned to irritation.

"What's that supposed to mean?" she muttered, half to herself, half to Natalie. "He's the one who has nothing to lose by waiting! He's just trying to frighten me. This entire thing is ridiculous . . . completely ridiculous!"

But Ramona's brave words and the disdainful toss of her head could not hide the tears welling up in her eyes.

Then, as if remembering herself, she turned to Natalie. "I want to thank you for taking the call." With an imperious gesture, she dismissed Natalie, indicating that she wished to be left alone.

Holding the precious orange chiffon over her arm, Natalie left the room quietly. And this time Ramona Martinez did nothing to stop her.

Chapter 2

The orange dress proved even more difficult to iron than Natalie had expected it would be. But she managed to do a beautiful job of it and, flushed from working with the iron in the poorly ventilated room, she stood back to admire her handiwork. She was sure that even the finicky Ramona would be pleased.

Natalie decided to take the dress up to Ramona's room immediately, even though it was only just after five. She hoped that Ramona would be out so that they would not have to speak. She felt certain Ramona had regretted her outburst and would prefer not to confront the linen maid to whom she had spoken so openly.

Natalie breathed a sigh of relief when there was no answer to her knock on the door of Room 215. Taking care to give the folds of the skirt one final shake, she hung the dress over the closet door.

As she left, Natalie's gaze fell once again on the exotic photograph of Ramona. Accustomed now to the resemblance between them, she briefly examined the photograph, searching for a clue to Ramona's character. Somehow she didn't believe Ramona was the casual socialite that the photograph—and the publicity she normally received—made her out to be.

Later, when she'd returned to the linen room and the other dresses waiting to be ironed, Natalie couldn't help pondering about Ramona Martinez. She seemed a strange mixture. On the one hand, spoiled, willful and imperious . . . yet on the other, friendly, generous and naive. Surely nothing could be seriously wrong? Probably she just had a taste for melodrama, Natalie decided.

She finished the last of her work for the hotel, then turned her attention to the dress that she planned to wear that evening. As she did so, she forced herself to consider something—or, rather, someone—whom she'd tried to avoid thinking about all day . . . Jack Steward.

Jack was an old friend. He and Natalie had grown up together and their parents had assumed that when the time came they would get married. Apparently Jack had assumed it, too. And, Natalie reminded herself sternly, it hadn't been until she had gone to school in France that she'd realized there was an alternative to her marrying Jack. Once she had tasted the excitement of life there, she knew that she didn't want to return to a small rural town in Sussex and settle down in a new subdivision with a Mini-Minor, two children and a husband called Jack Steward.

At first Jack hadn't taken her decision seriously. He had regarded Natalie's newfound independence with a mixture of playfulness and condescension. He had even teased her about her need to imitate men and sow her wild oats. But as the message gradually became clear that she meant what she said, Jack had become worried. Since then he had spent as much time with Natalie as his busy veterinary practice in a small English town would allow, coming to Paris for long weekends and spending all his other holidays with her.

Natalie hadn't been too concerned with his sudden possessiveness initially. After all, she'd reasoned, it was bound to take Jack a while to get accustomed to the idea that she wasn't going to marry him—especially since he'd assumed most of his life that she would. Because she cared about him and wanted to remain friends, she was willing to let him down slowly. But she was beginning to doubt whether that would be possible.

Jack's latest charade, his unannounced arrival late last night in Monte Carlo, had annoyed her more than she had let on to him. For she had made it perfectly clear to him in her letter that she regarded her working holiday in Monte Carlo as hers and hers alone, and that she would not welcome his company. Still, she thought now, it wasn't as if she'd been out on the town every night since her arrival. And Jack was so much like a member of the family that she couldn't bear to hurt him. It was just that she could never feel about him the way he obviously felt about her.

As she held her own dress up beside the gray satin one that she had finished ironing only moments before, Natalie sighed deeply. Although this was definitely her best dress, it looked a little sad in comparison with the expensive designer's original. The dress had brought her good luck when she'd worn it in the past, though, and there was no reason to assume it wouldn't bring her good luck once more.

Natalie could almost hear Jack saying, "You do wonders

for that dress, Natalie." He'd said it before and no doubt he'd say it again. There was nothing original about the comment, or about Jack, for that matter. But at least he was sincere and Natalie, remembering Fernando's broken promise to take her dancing, tried to convince herself that Jack's honesty and sincerity more than made up for his lack of flair. And he did mean a great deal to her.

Natalie finished the ironing and hastily put the linen room in order. She raced up the hotel's backstairs to her room on the second floor, where she changed quickly and began to arrange her hair, pleased that she'd taken the time to wash it before work that morning. As she undid the comb, her hair fell in thick waves far below her shoulders. She brushed it vigorously, its reflection gleaming back at her from the mirror. The simple summer dress she'd managed to buy at a sale in one of Paris's better shops suited her well. Close-fitting in the bodice, it emphasized her delicate waist, and the flared skirt flattered her long slender legs. It was her favorite color as well— which was what had convinced her in the first place that she had to have it. The rich moss green made her eyes seem even greener, and set off her delicate complexion perfectly. Maybe Jack hadn't just been *saying* that she looked good . . . maybe she really did, she thought cheerfully.

Natalie was finding it difficult, though, to get into the proper mood to spend an evening with Jack. She knew that if she let him, he would monopolize all her free time for as long as he stayed in Monte Carlo. But, she told herself, she shouldn't really complain. She could just as easily cancel her date with him and spend the evening reading some excellent but educational textbook.

In fact, the more she thought about it, the more she had

to admit that socially, Monte Carlo had been a bit of a disappointment. One evening, in an attempt to meet some people of her own age, she had gone over to the Sea Club. But the young man who had asked her to dance had stepped on her feet and had behaved so clumsily that she'd been relieved when a seventeen-year-old, young enough to be her kid brother, had rescued her. True, halfway through the evening a famous movie actor had walked in surrounded by what seemed like dozens of lovely starlets, but Natalie decided she would have had a better look at him if she'd been watching television.

A sudden honk outside the window let her know that Jack had arrived. She leaned out and called to him, "I'll be right down."

Deftly she put the finishing touch to her makeup, knowing that Jack would sit and wait for her quite happily. She hadn't wanted him to spend that time in her tiny living quarters; this space felt strictly private to her, and she'd managed to convince Jack of its importance. Besides, he always kept a magazine bunched up in his coat pocket for such an occasion and would bury his nose in it until she was ready.

Finished, she examined herself critically in the mirror, pleased that she had gone to the extra trouble. The soft tints of the makeup emphasized the delicate tan she'd begun to acquire after several hours of sunbathing and she knew that this evening she would look her best.

Jack confirmed her own opinion. He was watching the door eagerly as she came out and he let out a long low whistle when he caught sight of her.

"You know, Lili," he said, using the nickname he'd given

her years ago, "you're really one girl in a million! You can get yourself together in five minutes and look better than most do after hours in front of a mirror."

"How would you know about other girls?" she teased. "You haven't met enough to make a real comparison." She gave him a friendly kiss on the cheek and squeezed as gracefully as she could into the tiny car he had rented, hoping she wouldn't crush her carefully pressed dress in the process.

Jack leaned over and aware that he wanted more than the kindly kiss she had just given him, she gently pushed him back, saying, "Listen, Jack: I'm starving. Let's go and eat somewhere and then decide what we're going to do."

Although he couldn't hide the look of hurt that crossed his face, he smiled and said gallantly, "Your wish is my command."

His foot came down hard on the accelerator and the little Citroën took a convulsive leap away from the curb where it had been parked. It had been some time since Natalie had driven anywhere with Jack and she reflected that it was going to take her a while to get used to his rather erratic style of driving again.

"I know lots of girls," he said peevishly. Natalie's remark had obviously stung his male pride.

"Maybe you should make it your business to get to know a few more," Natalie said dulcetly. "Monte Carlo is filled with them. A good-looking man like you should have no trouble at all."

"I know what you're trying to tell me," her friend answered. "I've known for a long time. And don't worry, my dear, one of these days your fondest dreams will come true and some gorgeous female will come along and sweep me off my feet. Then you'll be rid of me forever, I promise."

Natalie looked at him sharply. Did he understand after all? Did he know that it could never work between them?

"As long as you promise me that whatever gorgeous female you end up marrying, you'll always keep in touch with me," she said warmly.

"I'm not about to let anyone ruin our relationship, Lili." Jack's reply was so gloomy that Natalie realized he was struggling to master his emotions. She looked at him affectionately, but his eyes were fixed firmly on the road ahead of them.

"Isn't this sea air marvelous?" he commented a few moments later. "By the way, what would you like to do tonight? Judging from that dress you're wearing, you weren't planning to lounge on the beach. Did you go swimming today?"

Natalie nodded. "This morning, around eight. The water was on the cool side, but it still felt great."

"You should have called me, Lili. You shouldn't swim alone that early in the day, even in Monte Carlo," he chided. "You never know what might happen and no one would even know where you were."

This was the relationship Natalie was used to, the one she felt comfortable with. Jack's concern was like that of a brother for his younger, slightly reckless sister.

"Oh," she said airily, "I knew you'd be exhausted after your drive from Paris. And besides, I swim most mornings when you're not here to look after me. What could possibly happen?"

In spite of the cramped seat, Natalie was enjoying the

ride. Suddenly she was no longer hungry. "Oh, Jack, let's just keep on driving. It's such a beautiful night and it's such a long time since I've been in a car. We can stop somewhere when we feel hungry."

"Sure, why not?" Jack turned along the road that followed the shoreline. The sun was resting on the edge of the horizon and the light sparkled on the water, tinting the waves with soft sunset colors, darkened in places by the lengthening shadows of the shore's rocks.

They traveled in silence, each sensing that the other was content to say nothing. They were constantly being passed by a stream of luxury cars, everything from Cadillacs and Rolls-Royces to Porsches and Maseratis, and every so often one of the drivers or passengers would give a friendly wave.

"What an old slowpoke this car is," Natalie remarked as yet another car passed them. "Don't you feel like an old lady, driving it?" she joked.

Natalie was surprised by his quick angry reaction.

"There's nothing wrong with this car, or with its driver," he snapped, giving the steering wheel a hard tug to the left. "I'll pass every one of those cars. Just watch!"

But just as the Citroën swung out, it moved directly into the path of a long, white American car that had also pulled out to pass them. Jack slammed on the brakes, but it was too late.

Natalie felt a sudden jolt, then the car took another leap forward, this time quite involuntarily. She was thrown violently against Jack before her head struck the steering wheel.

"Natalie . . . *Natalie!*" There was an edge of panic in Jack's voice. "Are you all right?"

Natalie wasn't sure what had happened. And she wasn't sure where she was. But she knew she was all right.

"Yes," she murmured. "I've got a bump on my forehead, though, I think. And," she added wanly, "I must look a mess."

Laughter reached her ears, and the sound of a voice that wasn't Jack's. "It would take a great deal more than a bump on your head to make you look a mess! But I do hope that it's nothing more serious than that."

Natalie opened her eyes. She was lying back in her seat, while Jack eyed her anxiously. A man had opened the passenger door and was crouching down beside her. Their eyes met, inches from each other. Very attractive, he looked at her with a smile that didn't quite hide his concern. Through a slight haze, Natalie saw that he was elegantly dressed in gray trousers and a black sports jacket.

"Oh, it was you then . . ." she said, still dazed.

"Yes. But I wasn't driving. My friend was and, as you can see, he's not too pleased about all this."

The stranger gestured with his hands toward a nearby vehicle. With a start, Natalie sat up. Yes, the man in the driver's seat of the white car was drumming his fingers impatiently on the steering wheel. Jack, realizing that it was only polite to apologize, especially since it seemed as though they weren't going to press charges, got out and approached the driver. Natalie could hear Jack clearing his throat.

"I'm very sorry about this, sir."

"That makes two of us," the driver replied. "You certainly have a most interesting style of driving."

"Your car doesn't seem to have been damaged at all." Jack's tone was relieved.

"No. Luckily not," came the pointed reply. "Yours, on the other hand, is," he continued. "Looks like your fender bore the brunt of our little mishap."

"I'm sure it'll be a cinch to have it fixed," Jack told him.

Natalie, still shocked, was drawn to the sound of the man's voice. It sounded vaguely familiar to her, although she couldn't for the life of her think why. Perhaps he had been a guest at the hotel? Anyway, she didn't feel like getting out of the car to investigate and it didn't sound as though Jack needed her. Besides, the stranger was still crouched beside her, blocking her exit.

She felt a slow blush spread over her face, for his eyes were telling her a great deal and in no uncertain terms. It was clear that she had made a very favorable impression on him. Fascinated, she couldn't turn away, even as with each passing second she felt more drawn, yet more troubled. Where had they met? A little shiver ran through her and she thought it must be an aftereffect of the accident.

"I'm glad it wasn't more serious," she managed to say at last.

The stranger smiled. Whatever he was feeling, he was certainly in control of himself, more than she was, Natalie thought. With his deeply tanned skin and dark good looks she didn't think he was French.

"I'm *very* glad that neither you nor your friend was hurt," he said courteously. His accent somehow reminded her of Ramona Martinez. Of course, that was it: she'd heard the same accent in the driver's voice; these men were Spanish, perhaps South American.

"Come on," the driver of the white car urged his companion. He was obviously impatient to be off.

"I'll be right there," the stranger called back. He made a

polite bow toward Natalie. She acknowledged the bow with a smile, then watched as he walked over to the car and got in.

Jack squeezed in behind the wheel of the Citroën and called out his apologies once more. The other driver, meanwhile, managed with considerable skill to pull his car free of Jack's twisted fender.

Natalie, pretending that she was checking on the condition of the white car, glanced back. Although she didn't meet the stranger's gaze, she knew that he, too, was watching her. And as the car passed them, she made a tremendous effort to appear calm. She fixed her eyes firmly on the driver, although she could also see the stranger through the corner of her eye.

For a brief moment Natalie allowed herself to imagine that she was being driven away in the big white car not by Jack, not by the man behind the wheel, but by the dark-eyed man. There had been a look of such kindness, of almost intuitive understanding in his eyes, that she was sorry to see him go.

"Well, that was a close call," Jack sighed. Natalie felt a twinge of pity for him, mixed with anger. With his crazily tousled hair and chestnut brown eyes he looked so young, so absurdly lacking in the sort of style that made the two men who had just driven away so distinctive.

"You're telling me," she replied. "What were you trying to prove, anyway? That you could have been a racing driver if you hadn't become a veterinarian?"

Chapter 3

The Citroën seemed little the worse for wear and neither Jack nor Natalie felt any serious aftereffects from the accident. They decided to continue their drive along the coast road, though Natalie privately began to long for the quiet and safe pleasure of a good Spanish novel. After an hour spent sitting on the rocks, talking and watching the lights come to life one by one along the shore, Jack suggested dinner at an inexpensive restaurant nearby.

In spite of all the excitement, or perhaps because of it, Natalie found that she had an excellent appetite. The meal was excellent, simple and well cooked, and as they drank a last cup of coffee, Natalie reflected yet again that a girl could do a lot worse than marry a man like Jack Steward. If only she could bring herself to feel differently about him!

But even as the thought crossed her mind, a startlingly clear image of the mysterious stranger banished it. Suddenly embarrassed, she blushed. To hide her confusion from Jack, she reached for her purse.

"It's on me," Jack insisted. "This is my first night in Monte Carlo and I'm in the mood to spend a bit of money. Maybe we could even go to the casinos and try our luck there?"

"Do we have to?" Natalie could not keep the apprehension out of her voice. One slip of fate in an evening was enough for her. . . .

"Well, don't sound so enthusiastic!" Jack laughed.

"I don't like gambling, that's all." Natalie was adamant. But so was Jack.

"Oh, come on! You're too young to be so set in your ways. Anyway, you know me. I hardly ever gamble, either, and I promise I won't get carried away. I can't very well come for a visit to Monte Carlo and never even put a foot in the casinos. It just wouldn't seem right."

Natalie nodded. She supposed Jack had a point. And she genuinely didn't want to throw a damper on his brief foray into the pleasures of Monte Carlo's night life.

As a matter of course Natalie had put her best dress on for the evening and she knew that she looked fine. She hadn't given a thought, however, to how she'd feel when the lights of the casino shone down on Jack's rather scruffy attire. . . .

At the casino, however, he didn't seem to notice a thing, but Natalie was angry at the doorman for the disapproving stare he shot at Jack as they went inside. And she was even angrier with herself for feeling embarrassed by her old friend's appearance.

The final straw came for Natalie when she saw Ramona Martinez, coolly poised at one of the large, round gaming tables. This was supposed to be her time off and she resented being reminded that during the day she was a mere linen maid. Quickly Natalie took Jack's arm and steered him away from Ramona. But they had to pass Ramona's table, and seeing that Jack had noticed the stunning girl, Natalie couldn't resist saying something to let him know she'd associated with the glamorous young woman—however slim their relationship was.

"That orange chiffon dress you see there happens to be one of my little triumphs," she said with a flourish. "I ironed it."

"No wonder that girl was the first thing I noticed when I came in," Jack teased.

"So, Señorita Martinez managed to catch your eye?" Natalie's voice had a slight edge to it that even she heard. Could she be jealous? And suddenly she realized that although it was all right for her to encourage Jack to take an interest in other women, she wasn't so sure that she'd actually like it if he did.

"She's a very beautiful woman." Jack seemed to sense that he was getting more response from Natalie than usual and, unwilling to lose his advantage, he continued to talk about Ramona.

"Of course she's beautiful, silly." Natalie was trying to turn the conversation around to its accepted routine. "It's high time you realized there are many other girls in the world—lots of them far more attractive than I am."

"There'll never be another one like you."

Natalie couldn't tell whether Jack was joking or serious. She was beginning to wonder who had the upper hand in this relationship, after all.

"Maybe that's just as well," she said calmly, determined to relax. She was sure that it was the atmosphere in the casino that was upsetting her. There was such an air of tension. Some people obviously liked it, she thought, looking around at the crowded tables. She certainly didn't. In spite of herself, she kept looking around for a tall dark figure. . . .

"You'd be much better off with the daughter of Arturo Martinez," Natalie continued, in an attempt to get her mind off the recent accident. Besides, she was curious about what Jack's reaction would be to such a statement. He didn't disappoint her.

"Arturo Martinez's daughter? She's his *daughter*?" He let out a low whistle. Laughingly Natalie shushed him.

"Not bad," he went on, ignoring her. "Maybe I should marry her. That way I could eat at better restaurants and I'd even have enough money to support you with."

"What are you waiting for?" Natalie said challengingly. "Marry her, why don't you?"

"Place your bets!" the croupier called out at the next table. The wheel began to turn.

"Well, are you going to play?" she dared her companion. Jack, now that he was actually in the casino and surrounded by the enormous tables, the elegant croupiers and the crowds of expensively dressed men and women, seemed a bit reluctant to try his luck.

"For sure," he replied, riffling through his pockets. "Put two hundred francs on the seven," he instructed the croupier.

"Two hundred francs on the seven," the man echoed.

Jack handed the croupier a thousand franc note and got a handful of chips in exchange. The wheel stopped.

"Thirty-one loses. Odd loses," the croupier informed, raking in the losing chips. Jack's were among them.

"Off to a good start, I see." Natalie couldn't resist teasing Jack.

But Jack was relaxed. "Don't worry. I'm bound to win sooner or later. Unless, of course, there's some radical change in my environment, like your falling in love with me or something." He looked at Natalie with an odd expression on his face. "Though I see I have nothing to worry about. Guess I can go ahead and play with the utmost confidence. Well, which one should I take a chance on this time?"

"Twenty-four; that's your age. Maybe you'll get lucky," Natalie said unenthusiastically. Jack tossed some chips on the twenty-four, then glanced up at the figure in the orange chiffon who had just moved to their table. One of the players had become discouraged and left; Ramona had wasted no time in taking his place.

"Tell me about Ramona Martinez," Jack whispered. "She's playing as though she's really hooked on the game. If that's true, I'd sure hate to be her father. You can lose millions here. Enough to hurt even a man like Martinez—or at least lighten his pockets, although I doubt any permanent damage could be done."

Natalie checked to make sure Ramona hadn't recognized her, but she needn't have worried. Jack was right. Ramona was playing with an absorption and an intensity that made her seem oblivious to everyone and everything—except the turn of the wheel and the landing position of the dice.

"You're wrong, there," Natalie said quietly. "I was talking to Ramona this morning and she told me her father's extremely worried about her gambling habit. She *is* hooked on it. So much so, in fact, that he's left her here in Monte Carlo with no money of her own to spend. He paid her hotel bill and left the hotel cashier in charge of her allowance. She has virtually no money."

"Well, for a girl with no money she's sure playing for big stakes," Jack commented. "She's just put down a heap of ten thousand franc chips. I think that your Miss Martinez was taking you for a good old-fashioned ride."

"*Messieurs, mesdames . . .* place your bets."

The croupier's voice possessed a hypnotic quality, Natalie thought idly. She watched, fascinated in spite of herself, as the wheel spun around again, this time coming to a stop at the red number seven.

"Wouldn't you know it!" groaned Jack. "And I had to switch to the twenty-four! I should have stuck to the seven. Once you've chosen something, you should always stick to it." He glanced at Natalie, and she knew he meant the remark to refer to more than just his style of gambling.

But Natalie was too busy concentrating on the heap of chips that Ramona had risked on the game to worry about Jack's hidden meaning. The wheel had stopped for the young woman as well, and it was obvious to any onlooker that she'd lost. Ramona's face was white and her lips taut as she watched the croupier's rake gather in a pile of chips that, from the look of it, represented a small fortune. She reached into her purse for more chips. They were the last she had, Natalie guessed, judging from the look on her face.

Jack, sensing that Natalie was more interested in Ramona's game than in his, turned to face the heiress. In an undertone he said to Natalie, "What was it you said about her, just a minute ago? Somebody's paying for this, unless she's been saving her allowance."

Natalie didn't answer immediately. She couldn't decide whether to tell Jack what she knew. Then she answered slowly, "I was wondering if she could have won the amount she bet on that last game this evening."

"No reason why not," Jack replied. "It certainly wouldn't be the first time that someone hit the jackpot."

"I just hope that that's how she did get the money," Natalie said. "Still, it does seem rather odd. Just this morning she was complaining that she'd scarcely a penny to spend."

Jack shrugged. "A girl like that wouldn't have any difficulty getting hold of some money. She wouldn't even have to try."

"Jack!" Natalie was shocked. "Can you seriously picture a Spanish girl from a family like hers—"

"Oh, come on, Natalie! I was only kidding. Can't you take a joke? Besides, you'd think I'd said it about you, the way you're going on."

There was some truth in Jack's remark, Natalie had to admit. She had leaped rather swiftly to Ramona's defense and for the second time that evening she found herself wondering why she'd got so emotionally involved with the Spanish girl.

"You're right," she agreed. "It's none of our business where she gets her money. I don't know why I got so worked up about it."

"Never mind," Jack soothed, adding, "It's probably no secret to anyone around here who her father is. With him in the background she won't have any trouble getting a loan. In fact, that's probably one of her loyal benefactors now."

As Jack spoke the croupier finished raking in the last of Ramona's chips and she turned around in her chair as a dark-haired man approached her. She held out her hand in a greeting that seemed to Natalie both defiant and desperate. She was saying something to him and he, bending down to listen to her, was slowly shaking his head. Natalie imagined that Ramona was employing all of her charms on the tall dark man dressed in an elegant velvet smoking jacket. But she wasn't having much success. Although Natalie couldn't see his face, she was sure that he was refusing her request. Sure enough, he shook his head again.

"I'll bet I know what she said," Jack remarked. He, too, was engrossed in the little drama being played out across the table. " 'I promise, this is the last time.' "

"You're probably right," Natalie conceded. The man was standing with his back to them now, but from the stiffness of his posture, it was clear that he was impervious to Ramona's pleas. Ramona looked utterly downcast—and at last he relented. He shrugged and reached into his vest pocket, then handed her two bills.

"Looks like ten thousand francs," Jack said incredulously.

Ramona's face was shining. She waved the man away. Now she had what she wanted it seemed that, for the moment at least, she wasn't interested in him. As he turned to leave her, Jack and Natalie were able to catch a glimpse of his face.

"I'd swear that was the guy—"

"No need to swear," Natalie interrupted. "It's him."

"The one that was driving that car I rammed into tonight?"

"Yes."

The driver of the white car walked past them, deep in

thought. So, Natalie decided, she had been right about him. He wasn't French. Seeing him with Ramona Martinez had confirmed her earlier hunch that both this man and his companion of earlier were Spaniards.

He *was* handsome, Natalie had to admit. And more importantly, he had real style. Because he'd stayed behind the wheel after the accident, Natalie hadn't had a chance to get a good look at him. She'd been too busy, she thought ruefully, admiring his friend. And again she wondered if he was also here tonight. But somehow she was certain that he wasn't. She'd have known instinctively if he were.

So, this was the man who had made the date with Ramona, Natalie mused, the man for whom she had had to 'look her best.' And now Natalie realized why she had recognized his voice. She had spoken to him on the phone that afternoon, and it had been the memory of that conversation, not the similarity of his accent to Ramona's, that had rung a bell for her earlier.

Ramona and her companion were still playing at the tables when Jack and Natalie left shortly after midnight. Although they had sat together at the same table, Natalie was sure Ramona hadn't noticed her. She'd been so obsessed with her bad luck, Natalie was certain, that she'd been indifferent to everything else.

Jack, however, was in excellent spirits. He had finally managed to put his chips on a winning number and left the casino five thousand francs richer than when he'd entered it.

"How about a drink?"

But Natalie was tired. And although she didn't want to admit it, preferring to put it down to the aftereffects of the accident, she felt vaguely depressed.

"No thanks, Jack," she said with a wan smile. "Save your money for tomorrow night. You'll need it to cover your losses."

"You're a great friend," he laughed. "Here I am, offering you a free drink, courtesy of my winnings, and you have the nerve to turn it down."

"I'm exhausted. Buy me a drink tomorrow night. Don't forget that I have to get up in six hours. And I'm covering for the other chambermaid as well."

Jack gave in as gracefully as he could. "All right, you win. I'll take you back to the hotel. And I won't even insist that you go swimming with me in the morning. But tomorrow night at seven sharp, you'd better be ready. We've got a date, okay?"

Natalie didn't really like the way Jack was planning to monopolize her time during his stay in Monte Carlo, but she was too tired to argue with him now.

"On one condition," she warned.

"What's that?"

"That you don't take me back to the casino."

"Not even to have the fun of gambling away my five thousand?" he persisted.

"Oh, that . . . leave that for later. You'll have plenty of time to lose your money, if that's what you want."

"Have it your way, then. Let's go."

ONCE SHE WAS BACK in her room, Natalie discovered that she wasn't able to sleep in spite of her exhaustion. She threw a light shawl over her nightgown and drew a chair up to the large window that faced the street. Although the hotel was within walking distance of the casino, it was far enough away from the main stream of the traffic to be quite deserted at this hour.

She sat and listened to the silence, enjoying the gentle night air perfumed with oleanders. She savored the peace, for in a few short hours she wouldn't have a minute to call her own.

Through a gap in the rooftops, Natalie glimpsed the moon. Carried by the summer breeze, music from the various night spots across Monte Carlo reached her in snatches that momentarily broke the stillness, then faded again. Her thoughts turned to the history of this famous city and all the people who had come here over the years. Many of them had written stories about their experiences, some of which Natalie had read, and most of them had had to do with love. She had love on her mind as well and for the first time in her life, the love she was dreaming about had a face now. It was a tawny face, dark and Spanish-looking; the man's hair was curly and black as night; his thick heavy brows shaded a pair of flashing eyes—eyes that glowed with a slow-burning flame in her mind . . . eyes that would disturb any woman, as they had disturbed her.

The strong firm lines of the mouth, the deeply cleft chin—everything about his face was energetic and virile—and it appeared to Natalie in the darkness as clearly as though the man to whom it belonged were actually standing before her.

The man I've been waiting for all my life.

The words, flashing through Natalie's mind, caught her

completely unawares. A shiver went through her, as it had at the time of the accident when he'd been bending over her. . . .

But now she knew what it meant and what it had meant then. Natalie deeply believed in the powers of human intuition, yet suddenly she was filled with despair. Surely a man of his obvious wealth and background would never be interested in a girl like her when there was a world full of beautiful, sophisticated women like Ramona Martinez to chose from? She was being foolish.

For no reason Natalie glanced down from the window. What she saw below startled her. It was as if her thoughts had managed to conjure Ramona out of thin air, for down on the sidewalk, clearly silhouetted in the light of a streetlamp, a young woman in an orange dress who could only be Ramona Martinez was walking arm in arm toward the hotel with a dark-haired man. Her voice broke the still summer night and carried clearly to Natalie's bedroom window only two stories away.

"Carlos . . . before you go, please give it back to me."

The couple had stopped under the streetlamp and Ramona had disengaged herself from her escort. The man she called Carlos stepped back a little.

"Give it back. Are you crazy?"

His voice was so devoid of warmth or tenderness that even Natalie was surprised. Ramona, too, was obviously shocked, for she took a step back. Her movement gave the impression that she was afraid of him.

"Carlos, you're being so cruel! Why, for God's sake? It wasn't so long ago that you were saying you loved me."

These words seemed to unnerve Carlos. He shifted

uneasily, almost as if he were trying to erase an unwanted memory from his mind, Natalie thought. Fascinated, she continued to watch, unable to tear her eyes away from a scene that she knew wasn't her business.

Ramona was no fool and, sensing a moment of weakness, she was trying to take full advantage of it. She sidled up to Carlos and tried to take his hands in hers. The expression on his face hardened. Perhaps he had been tricked by Ramona before? Natalie wouldn't be surprised. He took another step backward.

"Carlos, admit it," Ramona cajoled. "You said you loved me. And you are not a liar. I love you, Carlos, no matter what you think of me. You've got to believe that. You—" Carlos abruptly pulled his hands out of Ramona's reach.

"Get a grip on yourself, Ramona," he insisted, almost shouting. Natalie was suddenly nervous he might wake the guests and cause a scene. But Ramona had covered his mouth with her hand, and Carlos soon calmed down.

"All right," he said, removing her hand. "I shouldn't have shouted. But I'm sick and tired of all the stupid things you do! I've warned you again and again, Ramona: I told you that you'd spoil everything for us, and you have. It's too late now. And I hope you learn something from all this, because I'm leaving Monte Carlo and you won't see me again."

Ramona threw her arms around Carlos's neck, clinging to him desperately. Although Natalie could see that it was a struggle for him, Carlos pushed her away, although more gently than before.

"Think about what you're doing, Ramona," he said, his voice softer now. "Someone will hear us, or see us."

"I don't care!" Ramona cried. "Why should I care what people think about me? You're out to make a fool of me, anyway, aren't you? It should make you happy."

"I'm trying to cure myself of you, once and for all," he snapped. "And I'm trying to cure you, as well, although for all the thanks I'm getting, I wonder why I bother," he concluded bitterly.

"No matter how much it hurts me?" Ramona was in tears and Natalie realized that this was more than just a lovers' quarrel.

Carlos's reply was cruel. "No matter how much it hurts. You deserve everything you get."

"You're a brute!" Ramona shouted and Carlos, now as indifferent as she was about being seen or overheard, responded by reaching into his pocket for a cigarette. He put one in his mouth with an unnatural calm and started to light it. Ramona lunged. But suddenly she stopped and let her arms drop to her sides.

"Now that you've lit your precious cigarette, I want to ask you one more time, very nicely, to *please* give it back to me," she begged. "Even if you don't want to see me again, this is the least you can do for me, considering what we've meant to each other. It's the last thing I'll ever ask of you—I give you my word."

"So you can go out and make a fool of some other man? No, I'm sorry, dear Ramona, but I'm going to put a stop to you and your dangerous foolishness here and now. I meant every word I said earlier. You have exactly forty-eight hours. You can accomplish a great deal in forty-eight hours, you know. You already have. Now good night to you and good luck."

Carlos turned and slowly walked away in the direction of the town square.

"No . . . Carlos, wait! You can't leave me like this. You haven't even kissed me goodbye," she said suggestively. Ramona was obviously used to getting her own way, Natalie reflected wryly. Ramona, looking very lovely, stood in the light of the streetlamp, her arms outstretched and her eyes filled with tears. Carlos stopped and turned around. Ramona didn't move.

He walked back to her, gently putting his arms around her bare shoulders. She pressed against him and they melted together in a deep embrace. For a few moments they stayed there, seemingly oblivious to everything around them. It was hard to believe that they had quarreled only a few moments earlier and were saying goodbye forever.

Natalie, feeling she'd already heard and seen more than she should have, looked up and away out to sea where a passing ship cast a pool of slow-moving light on the water. But she looked down again quickly as Carlos shouted, "Bitch!"

Laughing nervously, Ramona took several steps back. In her hands she held a small object.

"Give me back my wallet," Carlos demanded, fury and hurt at her trickery lending his voice a menacing ring. "Don't be such a stupid fool! If you don't give it back to me, I'll call the police and have you arrested for theft. And we'll see how your father reacts."

Ramona let out a cry of fear, apparently believing Carlos. She handed over the wallet meekly and Carlos slipped it back into his pocket. Natalie felt sorry for Ramona. *Ramona is as gullible as a child*, she thought, *and Carlos is wrong to treat her so harshly.*

Once again Carlos turned to leave.

"And now, Ramona, if you're sure that you're quite

through with this ridiculous charade we can say goodbye."

Ramona said nothing; this time she didn't try to prevent Carlos from leaving. Her entire manner indicated defeat and she stood in silence watching him leave. Natalie's heart went out to her. She'd tried everything, done everything . . . and lost.

But Carlos wasn't finished. He walked a few paces toward the road, then turned to say, "It isn't in my wallet, anyway. I'd already handed it over to someone else."

Ramona's voice was incredulous. "You what?"

"I gave your check to someone else. You heard me the first time."

"Why, Carlos? Why?" Sobbing bitterly, Ramona turned and ran toward the hotel. Soon she disappeared through the front door.

Carlos gave a slight shrug of his shoulders and continued on his way to town. Natalie saw him light another cigarette with that same chilling calm, then he disappeared down the street and around the corner. Natalie drew the draperies shut, feeling uneasily like a voyeur.

She scolded herself roundly for having listened to Carlos and Ramona . . . but in spite of this, she had to admit she was intrigued. It was clear that Ramona was in trouble and that there was a check of some kind that she desperately wanted from Carlos. But just how serious, Natalie couldn't guess. She hoped that Ramona's usual inclination to dramatize had made the scene seem more important than it really was. Something, however, tugged at Natalie's instincts. She couldn't be sure how desperate Ramona was . . . or what she was likely to do to prove it.

Chapter 4

Natalie was fast asleep when a bell rang outside her room. It rang several times before she realized that it was the hall telephone, installed to wake sleepy hotel employees if they were needed by the guests for any reason. Natalie stumbled out of bed and answered in a drowsy voice that the night receptionist nevertheless managed to recognize.

"Natalie, it's Miss Martinez in room 215. She wants a couple of aspirins right away. You're on duty for Louise tonight, aren't you?"

Numbly Natalie pulled on her dressing gown. She took a bottle of aspirin from her own bathroom cabinet, for she didn't want to waste time getting them from the hotel supply room. She was sure that Ramona was terribly upset and that she needed the aspirins rather urgently.

"Come in," came the muffled reply to Natalie's soft knock. Natalie hadn't wanted to alert the entire hotel to the fact that Ramona was receiving guests at one o'clock in the morning. People were so nosy and eager to jump to conclusions, she thought, guiltily remembering the scene she'd witnessed earlier that night.

Turning on one of the side lamps, Natalie looked at Ramona. She lay motionless on her bed, completely hidden under a mound of tangled bedclothes. Natalie could only just glimpse a few wisps of her silky hair on the pillow.

"Set them down on the night table," a weak voice ordered. A delicate tawny hand then reached out from under the sheets. "There."

Natalie was about to leave when Ramona spoke again. This time it was clear that she had been crying.

"Would you be good enough to pour some of that mineral water into a glass for me?"

Natalie did as she was asked.

"Will that be all, madam?"

At the sound of Natalie's voice Ramona emerged from under the sheets and sat bolt upright.

"Natalie . . . it's you! I thought it was my regular chambermaid. I'm so sorry to have disturbed you at this hour."

As Ramona spoke she reached out for the glass of water. Her hand trembled as she lifted it and for a moment Natalie feared she would spill the water. She tried not to show Ramona how shocked she was by her appearance, yet Ramona seemed to sense what Natalie was thinking. She smiled faintly.

"Now you know why I was hiding under the sheets," she explained. "I've been crying and crying, and I must look perfectly dreadful by now! I had no desire to be gawked at by a curious chambermaid. I knew that she'd be spreading stories all over the hotel within five minutes if I gave her half a chance."

"You can relax, madam," Natalie said stiffly. "I have—"

But Ramona stopped her with a movement of her hand. "Oh, Natalie, don't be silly! Of course I didn't mean you. Why are you so sensitive? The minute I knew it was you I sat up. Could you hand me the aspirin? I feel as if my head is going to burst."

Natalie shook two tablets out of the bottle. She recognized the symptoms Ramona had just described all too well.

"Is it a migraine?" she asked sympathetically.

"Yes," Ramona groaned. "The worst one that I've had in ages!"

Natalie automatically took Ramona's pulse. As the eldest in a family of four children, she had learned to look after her brothers and sisters when they were ill and felt quite at ease now with Ramona. Her pulse, she discovered, was fast and her wrists hot to the touch. Natalie suspected that there was something more than just a migraine ailing the Spanish heiress.

"Did you catch cold tonight, madam? When did you start to feel unwell?"

Ramona made a vague gesture with her hand. "Oh, about an hour ago. I had a lovely evening at the casino but on the way back something very unpleasant happened." She struggled to maintain her self-control. She was still upset, and Natalie didn't want to say anything to her that might make her break down. She understood how proud Ramona was, because she was similarly disposed.

"I often get migraines," Ramona continued. "And I am susceptible to chills because of a heart condition I've had since I was a child. It affects my blood circulation sometimes. Oh, it's nothing serious, just annoying, and if I

overdo it occasionally I catch a chill and have to stay
propped up in bed for a few days. That's probably what's
the matter with me now."

Natalie knew there was more to it than the explanation
Ramona had just given her implied, but she didn't want to
intrude, so she just smiled sympathetically.

"That's too bad. Especially since you're alone and there
is no member of your family here to look after you."

"You're kind, Natalie," Ramona's eyes filled with tears
and Natalie was afraid that she just might break down.
"Thank you for your concern. I keep forgetting that you're
not on vacation like me. You have to get up early in the
morning. Go and get some sleep. I'm fine."

But as Natalie turned to go, she bent down and instinctively straightened Ramona's twisted sheets for her.
Somehow the gesture broke down what was left of
Ramona's composure. With a cry she grabbed Natalie's
hand.

"Oh, Natalie, I'm so unhappy!" she cried. She fell back
onto the bed and buried her head into the mass of pillows,
sobbing convulsively.

Natalie didn't know what to do. She was moved by this
outburst, but she didn't want the proud Spanish girl to
know that she'd deliberately overheard her conversation
with Carlos Vilar.

"Are you feeling worse?" she asked Ramona anxiously.
"Shall I call a doctor?"

Ramona shook her head, then reached out for a hand-
kerchief from the bedside table. She rolled over and lay
looking at Natalie as she dried her eyes and made an obvious effort to calm down.

"I'm so alone here. My father is traveling in the United

States on business and I have no one in Monte Carlo to confide in. Oh, I have relatives, of course, but one can't always talk to relatives."

Natalie was curious. "Why didn't you go with your father on his trip?"

"I wanted to stay on the Riviera. My brother, Eduardo, had planned to come and spend some time here, and a girl friend was coming as well. In the end, though, my brother went to Japan and my friend decided she couldn't leave her boyfriend, even for ten days."

Natalie was beginning to feel really tired and she wondered how she would manage to work the next day if she didn't get at least three hours' sleep. Once again it was as if Ramona read her mind.

"Do you have to go, Natalie? If you're not sleepy, would you stay here with me? I don't feel like being alone tonight. Usually I'm very independent but tonight is different. I really need some moral support," she ended plaintively.

Natalie knew that for a girl of Ramona's natural pride and privileged upbringing, such an admission of weakness to a mere linen maid had to mean that she was deeply upset. She really couldn't leave Ramona alone in such a state, she decided reluctantly.

"If you were an old friend of mine," Ramona began again, "I'd ask you for some advice."

Natalie was hurt. Abruptly, she had been put back in the position of servant. She couldn't keep a certain coldness out of her voice as she replied, "I'm sorry that there's no one here at the hotel whom you feel close to."

Ramona caught the injured tone in Natalie's voice, however, and responded immediately. "Oh, Natalie, I'm so careless! Please forgive me. It's not that I don't trust you

but we hardly know each other and I don't want to inflict
my troubles on you any more than I have already."

It was impossible not to believe Ramona's apology. She
was an odd mixture, Natalie reflected: imperious, spoiled
and vulnerable, and often all at the same time. But in spite
of herself, Natalie felt a growing affection for her. She
smiled and Ramona assumed that she was forgiven.

"Since I've been in Monte Carlo, you're the only person
I've met who's shown the least interest in me without it
having to do with the fact that I've got money," Ramona
rambled on. "I do trust you . . . and I need a friend
desperately right now. Can I rely on you?"

She looked beseechingly at Natalie, who was both
touched and cautious. She had spent enough time with
Ramona already to know how unpredictable she could be.
She hesitated now, afraid that Ramona might regret her
confession later and make trouble for her.

"You've got a fever, madam," Natalie reminded her
gently. "It would be much better if you tried to get some
sleep instead of talking. I'll stay with you for a while if you
like. How's your headache?"

But Ramona refused to be sidetracked. "Don't call me
madam, Natalie. You must be my friend. I have to ask
your advice and I can't unless you promise to be my friend.
Can't you see?" Her voice had risen slightly, and Natalie
began to fear that she might become hysterical. After all,
she'd suffered a few emotional disappointments that night,
something she was probably unused to.

"All right, then," Natalie smiled. "But be as quiet as you
can. These rooms aren't very soundproof and if the
management finds out I'm up here I could lose my job."

"Oh, if that's all you're worried about, you can relax,"

Ramona answered airily. "The couple next to me have gone off for a little trip to France and they won't be back for three days. As for the old lady on the other side, you can hear her snoring! She's the one who ought to be accused of causing a disturbance, not us."

Natalie was reminded once again how selfish Ramona was. *She can't even conceive of a world where the rules aren't made to suit her,* Natalie marveled. *No wonder she gets herself into trouble!* She seemed to think that everything and everybody would make an exception for Ramona Martinez!

"But you're right about one thing, Natalie," Ramona said softly. "I can't let anyone overhear our conversation. You see . . . ." Now that Ramona had convinced Natalie to hear her troubles, she seemed at a loss as to how to begin.

"Did it start at the casino?" Natalie asked.

"Yes, I gambled . . . and lost. I was playing with a lot of money. Far more than my father left me." Ramona stole a quick glance at Natalie.

"I borrowed the money," she continued, blushing. "When my father was still in Monte Carlo, I met a young man—the son of some very close friends of the family—Carlos. It was he who lent me the money tonight."

Natalie knew the answer before she asked the question.

"And this Carlos . . . is he the same Carlos Vilar who called you yesterday?"

Ramona sighed. "Yes, they are one and the same."

"Is this Carlos Vilar more than—more than a friend?"

Ramona's eyes filled with tears. "Yes," she said simply. "When I first met him, I thought he was the most handsome man I'd ever seen! He seemed so strong and athletic. Most of the men I've known are either smart or handsome.

He's both yet he isn't conceited. He's Spanish, too, which is important, and he loves excitement and challenge as much as I do. He races cars and motorcycles, and I used to love to drive with him! I'd beg him to let me drive, but although he was happy to take me everywhere with him, his answer was always no," she said wistfully. The memory of happier days with Carlos seemed to have brought a faint glow back to her pale cheeks.

"I found myself liking him more and more, wanting to please him. More than please him . . . ." Ramona's gaze met Natalie's and she blushed again. Natalie experienced a familiar feeling that Ramona was extremely young and inexperienced, despite her worldly airs. And again Natalie found it difficult to believe that a woman of her age could still be such a child in many ways.

"I knew that I was falling in love," Ramona went on, determined to tell Natalie the whole story. "At first, we went everywhere together. Oh, I couldn't have asked for a more agreeable or a more attractive escort. Everyone said that we made a beautiful couple. We dined together almost every evening, we went dancing together and to the casino. We were on the verge of deciding to spend the rest of our lives together. Then . . . ." Ramona choked back a sob.

"It's all my fault; I see that now!" she cried.

Natalie, who was feeling acutely older and more experienced than Ramona, poured her another glass of mineral water.

"Drink this," she ordered. "And try to keep calm. You'll only make yourself feel worse if you cry."

"Oh, I won't cry if only you'll stay," Ramona said eagerly. "I really believe that you can help me. Say that you'll help me, Natalie . . . I'm so alone and so frightened!"

"I'll help you . . . if I can," Natalie reassured her. She drew up a chair beside the bed and sat down, resigned to hearing the rest of Ramona's story. "So, basically everything between you and Carlos was going beautifully at first?" she asked encouragingly.

"Now that I look back on it, things were going too well," Ramona admitted miserably. "I don't know how I could have let myself be taken in by Carlos. I fell in love so quickly and I was blind to him! I've let him drive me to the brink of suicide!"

"Come on, Ramona. Aren't you being a bit melodramatic?" Natalie demanded, thinking longingly of her comfortable bed. Really, how could she possibly help this woman in her present overwrought state?

"But I'm not, Natalie. That's what's so terrible!"

Natalie couldn't help letting the impatience show in her voice. "Well, for heaven's sake, you'd better tell me what it is that you've done—otherwise we'll be here all night!"

"I signed a check with no funds in the bank," Ramona blurted.

"You had no money whatsoever in the bank?" Natalie demanded, incredulously.

"Oh, you can be quite sure that my father withdrew every cent before he left."

"But surely any bank in Monaco would advance you money? They know your father will return soon and will cover it for you."

"Natalie," Ramona said with deliberate patience, "you still don't understand, do you? You still don't realize how addicted I am to gambling, how much of my father's money I've lost already! He's so desperate that he'll do anything to make me stop this terrible obsession, including cutting me off entirely. And that's what he's done! He left the strictest instructions with the bank that under no circumstances were they to give me credit."

Natalie was silent. She was beginning to realize that this entire affair might be more serious than she'd supposed. . . or hoped, she thought uneasily.

Ramona was sitting up in bed now, her hands clasped around her knees. She was flushed slightly and the glow deepened the tones of her naturally rich complexion even more. Natalie couldn't help thinking as she watched the feverish girl that perhaps this Carlos Vilar hadn't been able to help himself. Perhaps he had fallen in love with the changeable Ramona against his own will?

"Ramona," she said slowly, "who did you make this check out to and where were you when you did it?"

"Carlos Vilar," Ramona answered in a low voice, averting her eyes from Natalie's gaze.

"He'd loaned me money on several occasions so that I could play the roulette tables at the casino. My love of gambling seemed to amuse him. He seemed happy to lend me the money—he has plenty—and asked for nothing in return. But as soon as my father left Carlos was no longer willing. One night, about a week ago, he told me that he'd never lend me money again!"

"But why would he change his mind so suddenly?" Natalie wondered aloud.

"Oh, I suppose it was because I was losing," Ramona sighed. "I've had the most incredible streak of bad luck recently. And I just couldn't believe it. I was certain it had to break and I'd win an enormous amount of money. You see, I had a dream—a fabulous dream! I dreamed I was driving away from Monte Carlo in a huge red truck, loaded high with piles of gold coins. I was laughing and laughing. . . ."

Natalie looked at Ramona, stunned. "You actually *believed* the dream?"

"Of course!" Ramona said promptly, her large eyes wide. "I believe in dreams, don't you?"

Natalie ignored the question. "What happened then?"

"Well, I told Carlos about my dream. He laughed but at me, not at the dream. Then he got very angry and told me he couldn't believe how stupid I was and how he had been crazy to get mixed up with me in the first place. Oh, it was terrible! And then he said that it was over between us."

As she recalled the events, Ramona became more excited. She began twisting her hands nervously.

"I wouldn't listen to him, Natalie. You have to understand what I'm like when I gamble. Nothing matters to me anymore. It's like a drug—and when its effects wear off I can hardly remember what I've said or done. I was so sure I'd win that night! Because of the dream, you see. I told Carlos that if he'd lend me the money just one more time, I'd pay him everything I owed him—and I'd never gamble again. He refused until I threatened to ask a complete stranger for the money. There are many men in Monte Carlo who would make such an arrangement—for a price," Ramona added, carefully monitoring Natalie's reaction.

But Natalie only indicated with a slight movement of her head that she understood Ramona's inference. She knew, too, that the girl liked to shock people, and that she was determined not to let Ramona think she had succeeded on that score.

"Carlos gave in. I wrote him a check for five hundred thousand francs and he gave me the money. I knew that unless I won that night, there would not be enough money in my account to cover the check. But I was wild with self-confidence." Ramona stopped, huge tears welling up in her reddened eyes.

"And you lost it all," Natalie finished. "Five hundred thousand francs is a fortune, or at least it would be for most people."

"I've compromised my father's honor as well. That is the worst thing. You may not realize, Natalie, what honor means to my father—a Spaniard and a product of a time when such matters were taken far more seriously than we take them today. I am his only daughter—his pride and joy! My mother died when I was little and he has raised me himself. Such a scandal, such a disgrace as this will cause him enormous grief and anger. I don't know which will be stronger and I fear them both."

It was on the tip of Natalie's tongue to ask Ramona why, if she felt so strongly about her father, she had behaved in such a manner. But the poor girl was suffering enough. It would be unkind to rub salt on a wound that was already bleeding.

"Couldn't you write to your father and tell him the truth?" she suggested. "Surely, if you promise never to gamble again, he will pay your debt?"

"No! He would not pay. And besides, the knowledge would kill him. My father has a weak heart. A shock of this kind on top of the pressures of his business would be too much for him."

Natalie tried another approach. "What about going to Carlos and asking him, out of his love for you, to give you back the check? If you absolutely swear to stop gambling, maybe he'd agree."

"I already have," Ramona said despondently.

"What did he say?"

"He said that now he understood that I had only spent time with him in order to bewitch him into lending me money! I told him that if only he would give me back the check, I would pay him back what I owed him. I promised to send him a bit of money each month out of the regular allowance my father gives me."

"I think that was a good idea. But he wouldn't do it?"

"No. He refused to return the check to me! He said he was going to make sure that I paid for what I've done. He went on about how all my life I've been protected from having to deal with the consequences of my actions. He was furious, and accused me of lying and cheating."

"Carlos Vilar doesn't love you," Natalie said firmly. "No man, however angry, however hurt, would behave as Carlos has if he loved you."

Natalie was surprised that Ramona didn't agree with her.

"Unless the person he loved did something so terrible that it killed that love. I think that's what happened with Carlos. He thought I'd made a fool of him. He is very Spanish, very proud. And now he is my enemy. I am terrified of him."

Natalie didn't know what to say. She wanted to comfort Ramona, to reassure her that Carlos would not cause her more harm. But she knew that Spanish men were, as Ramona had pointed out, often fiercely proud; any humiliation, particularly one inflicted by a woman, could indeed arouse in them the kind of passionate hatred

Ramona claimed Carlos now felt for her. She remembered their encounter in the lamplight: the cold stiffness of Carlos's attitude . . . his arrogance. Yes, that man could even hate the woman he claimed to love.

Ramona interrupted Natalie's thoughts impatiently.

"You haven't heard the entire story! You have to know everything if you are going to help me. For a week now, Carlos has been threatening to go to the police and have me arrested. We've continued seeing each other, though."

When Natalie raised her eyebrows at this remark, Ramona hurried on, eager to explain.

"I hoped that if we still saw each other he would realize his love hadn't died. I wanted him to give me back that check. We even went back to the casinos. And I gambled. I still hoped, you see, to make enough money on the tables to pay him back and end the whole mess!"

Natalie was shocked. "Ramona, after everything that had happened! How could you gamble again!"

"I don't know. I was desperate. And Carlos was willing to loan me money—indefinitely. The only thing he wouldn't do was give me back my check. I didn't understand; I still don't understand. And then last night it all fell apart. I lost again. But we had spent a lovely evening together and I thought he finally realized that in spite of my gambling he loved me too much to give me up. I tried to use my power over him—to get back the check. And suddenly he turned nasty. He told me that the matter was out of his hands. He'd signed the check over to someone else—a man he owed money to himself—a notorious blackmailer!" Ramona's voice broke into a sob.

"A blackmailer!" Natalie echoed.

Ramona looked at her in despair. "This man—his name

is Marco Ortega—will call me, Carlos said. I have to wait here until I've heard from him. Oh, Natalie, and Carlos has even left Monte Carlo! I'm all alone, in the hands of a blackmailer! And do you know what Carlos's last words to me were?"

Natalie shook her head.

"It's comforting to know that the laws are made for everyone . . . even the daughters of millionaires!"

Chapter 5

It was already light by the time an exhausted Ramona fell into a deep sleep and Natalie felt confident enough to leave her. She left a message for the hotel doctor before returning to her own room. If she didn't have time to sleep, at least she could refresh herself with a warm shower, she thought wearily. It was going to be a very long day.

When Natalie checked in later that morning to see how Ramona was, she informed her that the doctor had already been to see her. And he had agreed with Ramona's diagnosis: stress and lack of proper food and exercise had combined to undermine her health. But he had been reassuring, Ramona added. As long as she promised to get plenty of rest and stay in bed for a few days, as well as continue to take the medication he'd prescribed, she would soon be fine.

"As though I'm going anywhere," Ramona remarked glumly. "Little does he know that I'm as good as a prisoner in here."

Natalie was relieved to hear this. And Ramona was looking much better. Some of the color had returned to her cheeks and now that the maid had changed the sheets and drawn back the draperies to let in the bright morning sun, the room seemed completely different. Somehow Natalie felt Ramona would be able to cope with her difficulties. Last night she hadn't been so sure.

Natalie, though, was shocked at her own appearance when she happened to glance in the mirror beside Ramona's bed. In fact, of the two of them, she looked much the worse for wear. It had been an exhausting morning and she'd had so little sleep. There were dark rings under her eyes and her normally light skin was chalky white. She promised herself that before she went back to work, she would put on some makeup. The hotel guests didn't deserve to see her looking like this, she thought ruefully.

Natalie turned to say goodbye to Ramona, who was leaning over the bedside table, flipping through some papers.

"I'll drop in from time to time to see you, but I'm still a hotel employee, you know. I won't be able to spend too much time up here during working hours," she warned.

"Oh, don't be silly!" Natalie, more used to Ramona's reactions by now, smiled faintly. Such a selfish attitude wasn't surprising in someone, she decided, who had been thoroughly used to getting her own way and had never had to obey other people's wishes for fear of losing her job. Ignoring Ramona's protest, Natalie was about to leave anyway when Ramona stopped her.

"You must not go until you've read these letters," she insisted.

Natalie skimmed the proffered letters. The first was from Carlos. He had left Monte Carlo and wished Ramona good luck in her dealings with Marco Ortega. To a large degree, it was a repetition of what Ramona had told her the previous evening—except for the last sentence. Puzzled, Natalie read it out loud.

" 'Perhaps someday you will understand why I have done what I've done.' What does he mean by that?"

Ramona shook her head. "Nothing. Although, being a man, he would deny it, Carlos has a flair for the dramatic. Just like me. That's why we got on so well. It's also why we quarreled," she added tearfully. "He's just trying to defend his unforgivable behavior."

Natalie silently agreed. Dropping the letter on the bedside table, she picked up the other one. This one, Ramona told her, was from the blackmailer himself. Natalie was intrigued. What could a blackmailer have to say to his victim and how would he say it? The letter was in Spanish. It was written on simple, inexpensive paper and the pen had left blobs of ink scattered over it.

Natalie scanned its contents:

Señorita, I have just arrived from Nice. There I met your friend Carlos Vilar. As you know from your encounter with him last night, Señor Vilar gave me a check in payment of a debt.

Before I cash this check I wish to speak with you—in person.

Please meet me at the Yachtman, at nine o'clock this evening.

Do not feel you can avoid this meeting. And do not

send anyone else. Although I have used extreme restraint in this letter, others can tell you that if I am not obeyed, I behave very badly. Bring a newspaper and a rose. I would hate to mistake someone else for the famous Ramona Martinez.

Natalie folded the letter slowly. It was unsigned.

Ramona was weeping quietly. As she put the letter back on the table, Natalie bent down and impulsively stroked the unhappy girl's forehead.

"Please don't cry, Ramona," she said, touched by the real despair on the girl's face. "Speak to this man, Ortega. Tell him you're going to contact your father and get the money. He'll accept the delay. All he wants is the money. It's of no concern to him how you get it."

"But I can't." Ramona sobbed bitterly. "You still don't understand!"

In spite of her sympathy for Ramona, Natalie felt herself becoming impatient. Ramona seemed so unwilling even to try to find a way out of her difficulties. Natalie, used to looking after herself since she was quite young, couldn't fathom this defeatist attitude.

"Come on, Ramona," she urged. "Think for a minute. There must be *someone* you can go to. Perhaps another member of your family, if you don't want to tell your father."

Ramona gradually stopped crying. She sat up, staring thoughtfully at Natalie.

"Well, I could go to my brother," she said at last. "I could write to him. We don't see much of each other anymore since he became a doctor. And even if he doesn't approve of my behavior, he'd never abandon me to a blackmailer! Oh, Natalie, what a great idea!" Ramona's eyes shone.

"Well, for heaven's sake, why didn't you send him a telegram as soon as you received this letter?" Natalie demanded.

"I couldn't. He's on his way to a medical convention. But at least, I know he'll be in Berlin in three days. I can't reach him until then. He's traveling on his motorcycle and I don't know the route he's taking."

"Well, still, your problem is half-solved. All you have to do is to agree on a sum with Marco Ortega, then convince him that you can't give it to him until you've contacted your brother and received the money from him."

"That's all!" Ramona spat angrily. "You can be sure that with the father I've got, Ortega is going to demand a lot more than the five hundred thousand francs I owe Carlos! Oh, how could he have done this to me! I hate him!" she cried passionately.

Natalie was glad to see that Ramona was getting angry. She would need all the spirit she had in order to get through the ordeal ahead, she thought in sudden concern. An angry Ramona was far better than a weeping one— even if, Natalie reminded herself ruefully, the spoiled heiress was largely responsible for her own misfortune.

"There is one other way," Natalie said decisively. "You could try telling the blackmailer the truth: that your father won't pay a penny to get you out of this mess. If Ortega realizes that, he should be willing to accept whatever Eduardo is willing to pay."

"And be willing to wait until the money arrives," Ramona added.

There was silence as the two women thought over the dilemma. Finally Ramona nodded her head. "You're right, I've got to get in touch with my brother. It's the only solution. If Eduardo hadn't gone to the convention and I could contact him, I'm sure he'd come here immediately to help me out."

"Do you think he'll fly back here when he gets your message?" Natalie couldn't help her curiosity. She wondered what the brother of Ramona Martinez would look like.

"Oh, I don't want him to do that. If he just sends the money I'll be happier. I intend to tell him that I'm leaving Monte Carlo right away."

Natalie laughed. "Ramona, he won't believe you! How can you leave Monte Carlo if you're waiting for the money, with that check still in the hands of the blackmailer?"

Ramona bit her lip. "You're right. He'd never accept it." Then her eyes lighted up and she broke into a mischievous smile. "Unless, of course, I tell him that I've left everything in the hands of a trusted friend. You."

"Maybe. I somehow doubt you'll be able to get away with him not knowing how serious your difficulties are, but it's worth a try."

"Oh, Natalie," Ramona sighed, "I just don't want to worry him. I don't mind if he knows that I've gambled too much. I just would prefer that he doesn't find out that I've let a bad check fall into the hands of an unscrupulous man like Carlos. He'll be so angry at me for being so stupid. You see, Eduardo is different from my father. He doesn't care about the money. He just cares about me and it worries him that I'm so irresponsible."

Natalie could easily sympathize with Eduardo. Ramona must be the sort of sister who was constantly getting into scrapes and calling on her brother to help her get out of them.

She glanced sharply at Ramona. Although she didn't look as ill as she had the night before, she was still haggard and pale. A thought suddenly crossed her mind.

"By the way, you do realize that you won't be able to meet Mr. Ortega tonight?"

"What do you mean?" Ramona snapped. "Of course I'm going to meet him."

"But the doctor gave strict instructions that you stay in bed," Natalie protested.

Now it was Ramona's turn to be practical. "Really, Natalie," she said impatiently. "What else can I do? You know as well as I do that this man Ortega isn't going to accept a little excuse like stress. If I don't show up, he'll do something terrible—contact my father, or come to the hotel, or even get the police. I can't take any risks. Don't you see?"

"I'll go with you," Natalie said impulsively. "I'll be free by nine o'clock. That way at least there will be someone to look after you and you won't have to confront that dreadful man all by yourself."

Ramona looked at Natalie gratefully and smiled. "What a good friend you are, Natalie! I'm not sure I deserve such loyalty. I'm sure that fate sent you to help me. I don't know how I would manage if you weren't here."

"Do you really believe that it was fate that made me take a job as linen maid at the same time as you're a guest here?" Natalie smothered a laugh. There were obviously a lot of subjects on which she and Ramona differed and this was certainly one of them!

"Definitely," Ramona replied unperturbed. "It was so that you could help me when this awful thing happened, I'm convinced."

"Well, that certainly puts Ramona Martinez at the center of the universe, doesn't it?" Natalie remarked. "I'm not so sure where it puts me, though."

But Ramona only smiled. "Oh, it's too soon to tell. Who knows, though? Maybe I have an important role to play in your life as well. And no matter what happens, you know how deeply grateful I am for everything you're doing for me. I'll never forget it. You'll be able to count on me from now on, you know, Natalie."

Natalie felt embarrassed. Ramona might be spoiled and demanding but she was oddly good-natured; she hadn't even taken offense at the things she had just said.

"Oh, I haven't done anything," Natalie answered. "Except suggest you write to Eduardo and offer to come with you tonight."

"But you *know* you can't come. You read the letter. If Ortega sees me with someone else, he could do anything. I just can't risk it, that's all. I have to do everything just as he says, otherwise he won't be willing to wait until I contact Eduardo. Oh, Natalie, trust me! For once, I really think I know what I'm doing."

They both jumped as the telephone rang sharply beside Ramona. She cowered in the corner of the bed, all her fear returning.

"Please, Natalie . . . answer it for me. I can't bear to talk to anyone."

The call, to their immense relief, turned out to be for Natalie. Two of the guests needed their dresses ironed for that evening and the other girls were getting tired of covering for her.

"It's for me," Natalie whispered. "I've got to get back downstairs. But I'll be up at eight-thirty. The least I can do is help you to dress and see you into a taxi. Maybe I'll wait for you just down the street, in case anything happens."

Ramona gave Natalie's hand a grateful squeeze. "Thank you."

NATALIE HADN'T FORGOTTEN about Jack and she was waiting for him on the steps of the hotel as he drove up to collect her.

"Let's drive around for a minute, Jack," she said as she slid in beside him. "Then I'm afraid I've got to come back. There's something really important I have to do. Our evening's off."

Jack gave Natalie a genuinely despairing look.

"You mean you're going to break our date! Aw, Natalie . . . I've got three days in Monaco and I was counting on spending them with you." He looked at her accusingly. "There goes one of the three nights. . . . I'd like to know who's the lucky man."

Natalie was annoyed. He was a good-looking man and she often saw girls giving him the friendly eye. But he seemed to be interested in no one but her. It also annoyed her that he assumed that she would reserve all three evenings for him. After all, part of the reason she had come here in the first place had been to get away from Jack Steward. And he knew it.

But Natalie had no intention of telling Jack the real reason why she was breaking their date. Ramona had taken her into her confidence and she had no intention of breaking that trust.

But Jack surprised her. He pulled the car over suddenly and demanded, "What are you doing tonight, Natalie, really? Don't lie to me. Why not just tell me that you've got a date with another man. You know I love you enough to let you lead your own life. If you prefer someone else to me, tell me."

Natalie struggled to keep a straight face. If only he knew the sort of man that she had a date with!

"Relax, Jack. It's not a man. It's Ramona. I have to do her a favor. It came up suddenly."

"That Spanish girl in the orange dress?"

"I see you haven't forgotten." Natalie smiled.

"What does she need you for? Haven't you ironed enough dresses for her?"

"It's not a linen maid she needs tonight, Jack. She really needs a friend. She's all alone in Monte Carlo and she's in a bit of trouble. I'm going to help her. That's all I can tell you."

She leaned over and kissed him affectionately.

"Come on, cheer up. We've got half an hour. Let's make the best of it."

BUT IT WAS AFTER eight o'clock before Jack dropped her off at the hotel. Natalie raced up the steps almost colliding with the elevator boy inside.

"Have you changed rooms?" he asked.

Breathless, Natalie shook her head.

"Well, I think your friend is sick. The doctor just left. I took him down myself. He mentioned something about a fainting spell."

Alarmed, Natalie rushed to Ramona's room. The door was on the latch so she walked in. Ramona was awake and obviously waiting for her.

"Natalie!" she wailed.

"What happened?" Natalie asked. Ramona looked ill; there were dark circles under her eyes and the usually rich complexion was strangely pale and lifeless.

"I fainted. I was getting dressed and suddenly I had no strength. The doctor says it's nothing to worry about. I'm just under too much stress."

Before Ramona could say more, a nurse entered the room briskly.

"You're the young woman who needs the sedative?" She looked commandingly at Ramona.

"Yes," Ramona said weakly.

Natalie made a move to leave, thinking that the nurse would wish to be alone with her patient.

"Oh, there's no need to leave," she said, smiling at Natalie. She must have mistaken the expression on Natalie's face for concern about Ramona's health—which was partially true—for she added reassuringly, "Don't worry. Miss Martinez will be feeling much better in the morning. The doctor has said so. She's just a very highly strung young lady."

Natalie smiled back, trying to hide her anxiety. If only the woman would leave, and soon! Time was running out and somebody had to meet Ortega at nine o'clock. Suddenly Natalie felt a sinking sensation at the pit of her stomach. It would have to be her.

Ramona caught her eye and glanced significantly at the clock.

In a thinly disguised agony of impatience, Ramona accepted a sedative from the nurse. Natalie reassured her that she would make sure Ramona went to sleep immediately, and the nurse soon retired.

"Natalie," Ramona cried as soon as the door had shut. Her face was a mask of distress. "What shall we do? Look at the time!"

"I'll go."

"What do you mean? I told you, he said specifically not to send anyone in my place. You read—"

"Calm down and listen," Natalie ordered. "I'll go as you . . . as Ramona Martinez."

Natalie could see that Ramona was about to object. But suddenly the expression on her face changed. It became careful, calculating. "You know, it's not as farfetched as it might seem," she said slowly.

"Of course it isn't. We do look alike."

"That's not what I meant. It's a question of style. I'm quite well-known for the way I dress, you know. Ortega might have heard that I'm pretty flashy. But I think that my style—toned down a bit, of course—would work for you. Even friends of mine, if I dress you properly, might not recognize that it wasn't me. At least, friends of mine that I haven't seen for some time."

Natalie turned to the mirror and began to examine her reflection, glancing now and then at Ramona, who had got out of bed and was sorting through the clothes in her wardrobe. She brought over several dresses and held them up to Natalie, her finger on her lip, thoughtfully.

"If you were ten pounds heavier . . . and a little darker . . . .

Gosh, Natalie, it's almost uncanny how alike we'd look!
As it is, we're not going to have any trouble."

"Now, don't you start all your talk about fate," Natalie
warned. "Anyway, we don't have time. You've got to
make me look like you and I can't gain ten pounds in twenty
minutes—unless you've got any bright ideas?"

Suddenly a thought occurred to Natalie that she'd
overlooked.

"What about my Spanish?" she cried, panic-stricken.

Ramona was calm and reassuring this time. "You speak
an excellent Spanish. Your accent is very faint. I'm sure
that your family must have some Spanish blood somewhere. Even your coloring, though it's lighter than mine, is
similar. A little makeup and one of these dresses to accen-
tuate your curves and you'll look so breathtaking that no
one, least of all Marco Ortega, is going to sit back and
compare you point by point with me."

"But surely he'll have a picture of you," Natalie argued.
"Carlos probably gave him one. Have you been in the
papers lately?"

Now that she realized what she was getting herself into,
Natalie was becoming genuinely frightened. Accidentally
resembling someone was one thing, but deliberately imper-
sonating someone—and to a blackmailer—was altogether
different.

"No, remember what Ortega said in his letter. He's never
seen me. And I'm not in the papers regularly, Natalie, not
any more. My father discourages it. He dislikes publicity
of any kind and he says that, particularly these days what
with terrorists and social unrest, people in our station of
life should be discreet."

"Well," Natalie said reluctantly, "it is true that my

father's grandfather had some Spanish blood. But I didn't realize any of it had reached me. Except for my love of the language, that is."

"Oh, Natalie!" Ramona clapped her hands in excitement. "When all this terrible mess is over, we're going to have such good times together. You'll come and visit me in Madrid, and I'll take you everywhere to repay you for what you're about to do for me."

"Ramona—" Natalie was still not convinced "—do you really think that I can persuade him that I'm you? You're the daughter of a millionaire. You've traveled all over the world and you live a sophisticated life. I'm just a student from England."

Ramona laughed. "If you spent three weeks leading the life I've led you'd realize how superficial all that sophistication is. There's nothing you can't handle, Natalie. And anyway, you're meeting this man in a bar. It's not as if he's taking you to dine with royalty."

It was true. But then again it was easy for Ramona to say. Fate had been kind to her. She would remain safe in bed, probably asleep, throughout Natalie's ordeal. Natalie began to wonder seriously if there were more to Ramona's confidence in destiny than appeared on the surface. Certainly fate seemed to be looking after her.

"Natalie, I think this black dress is right for you. It's too small for me, but I always take it with me in the hope that eventually I'll lose enough weight to wear it again. I've had several photographs taken in it so if Carlos did give Ortega my picture it's likely that I might have been wearing this dress. That should help."

Natalie slipped on the dress and Ramona handed her a pearl choker and bracelet. "Here, wear these. And come over here; I'll do your hair and your makeup. You'll look fabulous."

But Natalie couldn't help worrying.

"Ramona, what if Ortega does notice my accent? I don't speak like a Spaniard, you know."

Ramona was surprisingly confident. "Your accent is perfectly acceptable, Natalie. I've told you. And don't forget that I've spent a lot of time in France and England, and in America, so it's understandable if *my* accent isn't perfect. I have lots of English-speaking friends, too. It's well-known that people pick up the accents of the people they spend time with. If Ortega says anything, just tell him that you've been with friends in England for the past few months. He couldn't possibly know it's a lie."

Natalie couldn't help noticing the tone of regret in Ramona's voice. She obviously enjoyed her reputation as a wealthy, beautiful heiress and when it came to questions of dress and makeup she was as self-assured as a girl with her background might be expected to be. Now it was Natalie who felt in need of instructions and comfort.

"You know," Ramona said as she made up Natalie's eyes, "you should let me dress you more often. You're like so many English and American girls I know. You're so—what's the word?"

"Un-put-together?" Natalie volunteered.

"Exactly."

Ramona admired her work. "Terrific! You look great. You're really beautiful, Natalie. Your air is different from mine, but apart from that, it's true that we could be mistaken for each other. It's a pity that I haven't something better in the way of jewelry. Unfortunately everything except my pearls is in hock."

Ramona imparted this bit of information with such indifference that Natalie raised her eyebrows in surprise.

"In hock?"

"Yes. But let's not talk about that now."

"Are you sure I don't look too glamorous, Ramona?" Natalie couldn't believe how uncertain she had become. All her prized self-possession seemed to have left her.

"Quite sure, Natalie. It's a modest enough dress. It just happens to be well made, that's all, and you're not used to it. The pearls are perfect for your skin," she went on. "They make it seem darker than it is. Under the circumstances, that's exactly what we want to achieve."

Moments later Natalie examined her appearance in the mirror. She had to admit that she looked elegant. Ramona was very skillful. Natalie now looked like a woman of discreet wealth; even to a casual observer in a town like Monte Carlo she would definitely not seem out of place. The dress was modestly cut, slender and clinging without being too revealing. The pearls did emphasize the soft glow of her complexion. Ramona had arranged Natalie's hair with great care and it curled softly around her face, nestling firmly at the back of her neck in a thick shiny loop. Complete with a close-fitting black coat and delicate high heels, she had to admit she looked every inch an heiress.

Trying to keep the fear out of her voice, Natalie said, "Well, I'd better not keep Mr. Marco Ortega waiting. Pray for me. I'll need it."

Ramona put her arms protectively around Natalie.

"Don't worry. You'll be safe enough. That man's going to think twice before doing anything to the daughter of Arturo Martinez."

Natalie shuddered. "Provided that he believes I really am his daughter! What if he suspects something?"

Ramona shrugged. "How could he? He said in his letter to bring a newspaper and a rose so that he could identify you. Natalie, we've been through this. Take one of these roses. Carlos sent them. And here's this morning's paper. You'll be fine."

Natalie was halfway out the door when Ramona suddenly cried out, "Oh, I almost forgot! Take my handbag. It has everything in it: credit cards, money and my cigarette case with my initials. If you make sure to open it from time to time to take things out, he'll be more likely to think you're me."

"You think of everything," Natalie replied. "Perhaps the next time you get yourself in a fix, you'll think ahead."

"If you get a taxi immediately, you should be there just in time," Ramona answered. "And Natalie . . . thank you."

With a sigh of resignation, Natalie slipped into the hallway. She had no intention of taking a taxi from the front lobby. All the bellhops knew her and in her glamorous outfit she would be sure to arouse their curiosity. No, she would walk across to the corner of the boulevard and hail a cab from there.

Chapter 6

Natalie was relieved to find that the Yachtman bar was a simple place. A clock on the wall chimed nine o'clock just as she entered. It was almost, she thought to herself, as if fate really were taking a hand in the entire affair. Again she found herself wondering if Ramona was right to believe in fate.

The ride in the taxi had been nerve-racking. It had taken all of Natalie's self-control not to tell the driver to take her back to Monte Carlo. As he had turned away from the city and onto the coastal road that led toward Menton, Natalie had felt panic grip her. Anything could happen. She might never even return from her encounter with Ortega.

But the worst moment of all had been watching the taxi as it finally disappeared from sight. Natalie had had to force herself not to run after the driver. And she still wasn't sure why she hadn't. It would have been a perfectly understandable action. After all, she had known Ramona

Martinez only a few hours. What did she owe her that she was willing to risk her life for her?

But Natalie knew that somehow her decision to meet Ortega had to do with why she had come to Monte Carlo in the first place. It had to do with her decision not to marry Jack Steward, to become a diplomat. She'd been longing for some adventure: wasn't this the perfect opportunity? And if she accorded herself well, there was every reason she would return safe and unharmed—and successful.

The bar was well lit and had a friendly air. The two bartenders and the plump lady in charge of the cash register all smiled at her as she entered. Natalie comforted herself with the thought that she would be able to rely on them if Ortega began to play rough. She listened to the cashier's softly accented French with a linguist's pleasure. Even if she hadn't known where she was, the woman's almost Italian sounding speech would have told her she was in Provence.

Natalie was just as reassured by the clientele as she had been by the bar's employees. People were scattered around the room in such a way as to dispel Natalie's worry that Ortega might have brought a number of his comrades along to support him in the case of any unpleasantness. These people were just too decent-looking to be involved with a man like Ortega, or so she imagined.

Only three of the men in the bar were sitting alone and, her heart suddenly in her mouth, Natalie examined them as unobstrusively as she could as she strolled over to a table.

One man was about fifty and graying at the temples. He smiled at her rather knowingly but Natalie paid no attention. She hadn't been working at the Hotel de Paris for almost a month for nothing. She knew what that look meant and she dismissed the man as harmless. Besides, he looked too middle-class and married to be a blackmailer. Blackmailers, she decided, occupied a class of their own.

Natalie was pleased to see that her judgment had been accurate. At that moment an attractive woman emerged from the ladies' restroom and joined the man at his table. From the way they behaved, Natalie thought, he probably was her husband. Gripping the newspaper in her hand, she continued in search of a table. She wanted to be as close to the other patrons of the bar as possible, and was glad she had arrived before Ortega. She was sure *he* would have chosen a table as far away from everybody as possible.

"Another beer, please, bartender," a pale fair-haired man called out in a broad American accent. Natalie breathed another sigh of relief. He couldn't possibly be Ortega. Two down and one to go, she thought.

The third man was bent over his newspaper. He seemed so absorbed in it that Natalie assumed he hadn't noticed her arrival. But she had noticed him. He was nattily dressed and even seemed handsome. His hair was dark and curly and a slim powerful hand extended gracefully from the elegantly turned cuff of his blazer. In spite of her predicament, Natalie was curious about him.

There was nothing to do now but find a table and wait. She chose one near the far side of the bar, in direct line of sight of the friendly cashier. She set the newspaper down conspicuously on the table top and sat down.

"Would *mademoiselle* like a drink?" Natalie looked up nervously. One of the two men who had been behind the bar as she entered now stood before her.

"Coca-Cola, thank you. I'm waiting for someone."

As she spoke Natalie thought she saw the man reading the newspaper give a start. He turned in her direction and her heart almost stopped. It couldn't be! Somehow she managed not to cry out or make any move that would betray her, but she could feel the blood rushing to her cheeks.

Suddenly it became painfully clear. The white car . . . the Spaniard at the wheel whom she now knew was Carlos Vilar, Ramona's ex-boyfriend. And the man with him. Of course, it would make sense that he was the blackmailer to whom Carlos had given Ramona's check. And here he was.

But Natalie's heart rebelled. Surely not! She had already decided how the blackmailer would look. He wouldn't have the soft flabby appearance of the middle-aged man who'd eyed her when she'd entered the bar. On the other hand, he certainly couldn't possess the high aristocratic forehead, the laughing eyes and the refined air of Carlos Vilar's driving companion.

Natalie dug her fingernails into the palm of her hand so hard that it almost hurt, praying that he wasn't Ortega, that he was here merely by coincidence and, recognizing her, was coming over to say hello. For he was coming over. She could hear the scraping sound of his chair as he pushed it back.

Her thoughts were racing out of control. Why should a man who looked kind and decent necessarily have to be kind and decent, she wondered, fearing the truth. She was old enough not to nurse such illusions. She had to accept her error, had to ignore the feelings that this man aroused in her. Because he was a common criminal. He was standing beside her now and bowed. "Excuse me, *señorita*. But it was you I met last night? Around seven o'clock." He smiled and once again Natalie noticed how white his teeth appeared in his deeply tanned face. "Or perhaps I should be a bit more blunt. Wasn't it your boyfriend's yellow car that ran into my friend's white one?"

Natalie smiled nervously. "He's not my boyfriend. He's just a friend."

Desperately she wished that he was just Carlos Vilar's friend, nothing more. She even began to believe it.

"I trust that you have fully recovered from the accident?" he inquired politely. "I don't see the slightest sign of that bump on your forehead that you were so worried about. In fact, you're looking particularly well."

Natalie blushed. But she knew it was true. The taxi driver and the people in the bar had all gawked at her with undisguised admiration. Now she was glad Ramona had insisted she dress so well.

"I'm fine, thank you," she said, ignoring the compliment. "Was your friend angry? Were you late getting to Nice?"

The Spaniard didn't answer immediately. The look in his eyes was even more disturbing now than it had been the night before. Suddenly, he frowned, as if trying to remember what she was referring to.

"He was furious," he said a moment later, the frown vanishing. "We were late, but it doesn't matter. After all, it gave me the opportunity to meet you. May I sit down?"

Natalie hesitated. She wanted to talk to this man more than anything in the world, yet she knew that at any moment Ortega would walk into the room. This man's presence would startle him and he might think she had disobeyed his instructions. She couldn't jeopardize Ramona's future.

The stranger, quick to sense her hesitation, drew back. "You are waiting for someone? Ah, that's what I was afraid of. And judging from the look on your face he must be the insanely jealous type."

Fear that he would leave made Natalie bold. "What about you?" she asked. "Is the lady you're waiting for late as well?"

As soon as she'd uttered the words, Natalie was shocked to discover that she was jealous, jealous of any woman who knew this man. And she didn't even know his name.

"What makes you think that the person I'm waiting for is a woman?" he laughed. "Do you take me for some sort of Don Juan?"

Too confused to speak, afraid that whatever she said would give her away, Natalie was silent. But when the stranger made to leave, she couldn't help herself.

"Perhaps we'll see each other again?"

"What would be the point?"

The reply was quick and Natalie froze.

Suddenly he leaned down. He was about to kiss her hand and she felt her heart skip a beat. She avoided his gaze but could still see the gleam of the gold buttons on his blazer.

The stranger seemed to stiffen, as if in response. Instinctively Natalie glanced up, her shyness forgotten. Had the woman he'd been waiting for finally arrived? But no, he was staring oddly at the newspaper, his face a mask of bewilderment. Then he straightened and looked at her questioningly. He picked up the paper and indicated the rose lying next to it.

"Are these yours?" he inquired.

Natalie could scarcely breathe. With those words a wonderful dream—a dream that had only just begun—ended. She saw that the lines of his mouth had grown hard. Afraid of what he would say now, she spoke quickly.

"Who are you?" But it was only a formality. She knew the answer.

"My name is Marco Ortega," he said softly. And then, in sudden anger, he threw the newspaper down on top of the rose, crushing it. Again he leaned over the table, staring hard at Natalie. But this time his eyes were full of accusation. "Surely you're not going to tell me that you're Ramona Martinez?" he demanded.

Natalie knew that if Ramona were to come out of all this unharmed, now was the moment to begin to play her part.

"Of course I am Ramona Martinez, the daughter of Arturo Martinez," she answered coolly. "Does that strike you as so extraordinary, Mr. Ortega? After all, you are responsible for setting up this entire affair. Or have you forgotten? Shall I show you the letter you sent me, to refresh your memory?"

As Natalie rummaged through Ramona's handbag for the letter Ortega's expression grew even more troubled. He waved the letter aside.

"Well, now that we've introduced ourselves, let's get down to business. But before we begin, Miss Martinez—" Ortega pronounced her name so deliberately and with such scorn that Natalie trembled "—I want to tell you how genuinely sorry I am that Ramona Martinez turned out to be the lovely young woman in the yellow car. After all," Ortega paused as he searched in the pocket of his blazer for a cigarette, "I've got a good reason to be surprised. It is most unusual to find the daughter of a millionaire running around in a crate like that—and in the company of a man who looks as though he's been picked out of the cheering section for a college ball game."

Natalie took a deep breath. She hated him for insulting Jack. But if she were to convince him that she really was Ramona Martinez, she would have to beat him at his own game. Natalie feigned surprise and disapproval that anyone should question her behavior.

"Really, Mr. Ortega," she drawled. "I'm rather fed up with expensive cars and wealthy men who can't seem to make it through an evening without wanting to make love to me. Jack and his jalopy were a refreshing change."

"I didn't set up this meeting to discuss your choice of cars or companions," he replied.

Determined not to let Marco Ortega get the better of her, Natalie continued, "I didn't think so. Why don't you just tell me what you want? Then we can settle this entire affair."

"I am glad to see that you are prepared to do business. I assure you that I had a good reason for inviting you here. I have in mind—"

"Money, of course," Natalie finished. "What else would a man like you want with someone like me?"

Marco's jaw contracted. "What else do you think I might want from the daughter of one of the richest men in Europe?" He looked at her so frankly that Natalie had to turn her head away. She was furious with him—and with herself—for beginning to blush at the suggestive remark.

"What a pity," Marco went on, "that the charms I see displayed before me did not come in the person of an ordinary young lady: a working girl, for instance, or a student on holiday." A hint of a smile curled at his lips.

"Such a girl would lack the experience to see through you," Natalie answered, fervently hoping he wasn't referring to herself.

"Oh, who knows what might have happened between a man and woman who'd met under normal circumstances?" Ortega shrugged, evidently bored. "Bartender!" he called. "Bring my drink over here." Natalie watched the bartender as he carried over Marco's drink from the bar to their table. She took advantage of this little break in their conversation to gather her thoughts. She was here to get Ramona's check from this man. Why was she finding it so hard to keep that in mind?

"Have you got the money to cover the check?" Ortega asked abruptly.

Natalie assumed a despairing look she knew the real Ramona would have given Ortega. "I haven't got it quite yet. But I will very shortly. I've informed my brother and he'll send me the money as soon as he can."

Ortega was surprised. "Where is your brother now?" As his eyes fixed themselves on her, Natalie shifted uncomfortably, but she stared back at him with a level gaze.

"I don't know. I won't be able to reach him until a few days."

"A few days?" he repeated.

If only he would accept the delay, Natalie prayed. She

could feel her body tense with nervousness. "Yes, that's right," she said as calmly as she could. "I am asking you to wait for three more days."

"And what makes you think that I'll wait three days for the five hundred thousand francs you owe me, Miss Martinez?" Ortega leaned across the table and looked at her intensely. In spite of her fear, Natalie couldn't help wondering what it would be like to have those same eyes staring at her out of love, not hostility. Hastily she shoved the thought aside.

"I can only hope that you will," she answered. "It's the best I can do."

Marco lighted the cigarette he had been holding in his hand for some time. Only after he had begun to smoke, though, did he think to offer one to Natalie.

"I don't suppose you want a cigarette?"

"Extortion doesn't require politeness," she replied sharply. "But most men would have at least had the courtesy to offer me one."

Ortega, however, was imperturbed. He looked her up and down again, with the same cold, calculating look. Only this time, it seemed to Natalie, he was not estimating her physical charms but her financial ones. She was sure he was figuring out just how much money he would be able to get from her.

"I'm not a particularly polished individual," he said in a tone that made it clear she should not mistake his words for an apology. "What do you expect from a man with my . . . ah, reputation?"

"Some pirates have charming manners," Natalie replied. At first she thought Ortega was going to get angry and she scolded herself. She was going to ruin everything if she didn't watch her tongue!

Ortega, though, surprised Natalie by bursting out laughing. "You must be an amusing young woman under normal circumstances," he chuckled. "You're funny even now and you can't possibly be feeling very relaxed."

But before Natalie could reply, Ortega's face had again grown serious. "Let's get things straight, Miss Martinez. You say that you'll have the money in three days' time. But have you considered that by making me wait for money that by rights is mine, you're causing me considerable inconvenience? And you're also depriving me of the interest I could be earning on the money? So, don't you think that some compensation for such a loss is in order?"

Natalie looked scathingly at Ortega. "Naturally I've thought of it," she retorted. "Just exactly how much do you estimate this 'loss' would come to?"

"Oh, let's say double the value of the check. Would you be agreeable to that?"

"Double? Do you mean the original five hundred thousand francs plus one million more?"

"Precisely."

Natalie was stunned.

"Are you the daughter of Arturo Martinez or aren't you?" Ortega said firmly.

Natalie's heart began to pound. But she quickly realized that Ortega was referring to Ramona's family's wealth. He was not suspicious of her identity . . . or was he?

"There are certain things you should know," she said, trying to gain control of the conversation. "I cannot possibly go to my father and tell him about this matter. It would be disastrous for me—and useless for you. If my father knew what I've done he would watch me go to jail before spending a single cent to cover my debts."

"Doesn't your father love you, Miss Martinez? I understand he does."

"I don't care what you've been told! The fact of the matter is that while he adores me—" and here Natalie's voice quavered precisely as Ramona's would have "—he's unwavering in his principles when it comes to the family honor. He would pay you the exact amount of the check, if he had to, but not a penny more—and only after a scandal. I've gone against my father one too many times to count on him now, Mr. Ortega. And I stress, you would receive only the exact amount of the original check. Not a penny more. There would certainly be no 'compensation' as you put it. I advise you, therefore," Natalie finished, proud of her performance, "to accept my offer. It is the best you will get."

Ortega was silent for a few minutes. Then he lit another cigarette and looked at Natalie. "What you say may well be true," he said. "But your brother has money. And normally you do as well. Surely, between you, you will be able to come up with the modest sum I've requested." Then abruptly his tone changed. "I have complete confidence in you and your brother, Miss Martinez. You will pay me one and a half million francs and you will pay it within four days."

Now Natalie knew that Ortega had just been allowing her the illusion that she was in control. This was Ortega's game and she had no choice other than to go along with it. And on his terms.

"If I do as you say," she said in a haughty voice, "will you give me back that check?"

"Of course. I'm not a complete villain, you know. Especially when I'm dealing with such an attractive young woman." Again his look was openly sensual. Natalie seethed. How dare he treat her so disrespectfully? But, she reminded herself sternly, Ortega's manners were not the point at hand. She *had* to get that check back.

"Four days," she said. "It's not much time."

"It may not seem like a long time to you, Miss Martinez," Marco replied, "but it's a long time for me. I may even find myself getting bored. And therefore, I have one more condition: if you will guarantee me the pleasure of your company for some portion of each day until the check arrives, I will agree to our little deal." He smiled at her, curious to see how she would react to his proposal.

If it was a strong reaction he wanted, Natalie didn't disappoint him.

"Keep you company!" she exploded. "Don't you think that your demands are getting a little out of hand, Mr. Ortega? Why should I keep you, a common blackmailer, company just because it is taking me a few days to satisfy your greed?"

"My dear Miss Martinez—" Ortega's eyes had narrowed and there was an edge to his voice that sent an involuntary shudder through Natalie "—may I remind you that while I am in the habit of asking for what I want, I am equally capable of taking it? Business is business, and I am determined to reassure myself daily that you haven't skipped town before the money is safely in my hands. The easiest way to make sure of that is to meet you here each evening at the same time. And let me warn you: you should take these appointments very seriously indeed. For if you should fail to show up some night, I will assume that you have left Monte Carlo and I won't hesitate to go straight to the bank with your check—and with the signed note from Carlos authorizing them to transfer the funds to me. Do I make myself quite clear?"

It was all Natalie could do to restrain herself. But, like it or not, she knew she was in his power. Anything she might do now could result in Ortega's making even greater demands later. She couldn't resist one comment, however.

"Has it not crossed your mind, Mr. Ortega, that I might have made other plans for my evenings in Monte Carlo?"

Marco smiled.

"What plans could you possibly have that would appeal more to you than meeting me here at the Yachtman?" he said smoothly, his lips twitching. "I'm quite aware that because of the rather . . . unusual nature of my occupation you might not expect me to be the most agreeable of companions," he continued. "However, I can assure you that I'll do everything possible to show you the more attractive side of my personality."

Ortega was laughing at her! He had her completely in his power and he knew it. Natalie turned her head so he wouldn't see the tears in her eyes.

"And if, heaven forbid," Ortega went on, obviously enjoying his position, "you should still insist that my company is not particularly to your liking, you will at least have the good grace to admit that it's a very mild punishment for the crime you have committed. For it is a crime. You used your position as Arturo Martinez's daughter to play—and I use the word deliberately—with other people's pesetas, didn't you?"

Natalie was blushing to the roots of her hair. She felt as though she, not Ramona, was being accused. And she had to admit that, however distasteful his own behavior, Ortega was right. Ramona had behaved very badly and was relying on her wealth to get her out of trouble. But even worse than that, Natalie found herself wanting to confess everything. Shocked and ashamed to discover that she cared what this man thought of her, that she wanted him to know she was innocent, she struggled against telling the truth. For in spite of his elegant clothes and stylish manner, Ortega, she thought bitterly, was nothing more than a common thief.

If Marco had not stood up at that moment, Natalie might have given in to her mad desire. But he obviously felt that everything had been said and seemed anxious to leave.

"So, every evening for the next four days we will meet here at nine o'clock sharp," he instructed. "I have my car. Do you want a lift back to the hotel?"

Natalie shook her head. "No. The fact that I am forced to meet with you here doesn't mean that I intend to spend a minute longer in your company than I have to."

"Just as you like," Ortega replied curtly. "You're not afraid of me, are you, Miss Martinez?"

Natalie met his gaze head-on. "What reason do I have to trust you?" she accused.

"Sometimes people trust each other for no good reason, that's all." His reply was surprisingly gentle and that, more than anything, almost destroyed Natalie's determined composure. As long as she and Ortega continued to needle each other, she felt she could handle the situation. Any kindness would destroy her careful mask within five minutes.

"Mr. Ortega, in this case to trust you would be to fly in the face of reason."

The expression on Ortega's face became stony and Natalie wondered if she'd gone too far this time. Perhaps there was an outside chance that he really was softening, that he would let her—Ramona Martinez—off the hook and this entire miserable charade could end. But no, she concluded, he was a blackmailer through and through. He wasn't the sort of man to do young ladies favors for sentimental reasons. Especially wealthy ladies like Ramona. Still she had nothing to lose by at least being civil to him, she reasoned.

"Frankly," she tried again, "I don't think it's a good idea for the guests or the employees of the hotel to see us together."

"You're quite shrewd, aren't you?" Ortega gave her a strange look that Natalie couldn't interpret. "And you're right. I'll say good-night now, Ramona, and see you tomorrow."

At the sound of Ramona's name, Natalie started slightly. Ortega noticed.

"Does it bother you so much to be called by your first name? That is your name, isn't it?"

Natalie was on her guard again and decided that she'd better attack head-on. If she wasn't careful, the whole game would be over.

"You know perfectly well, *señor*, that I am not accustomed to total strangers addressing me by my first name."

"Oh, come now, Miss Martinez! Me, a stranger! I'm Spanish, after all, and besides, I'm lending you a rather large sum of money."

"Lending?" Natalie couldn't keep the shock out of her voice.

"Yes, lending. For four days at least." Ortega's voice was once again cool and businesslike. "Now, no more nonsense. I'm going to call you Ramona. I like the sound of it and it suits you. As for you, I don't give you permission to call me Marco—I *insist* upon it!"

"You *insist*?" Natalie inquired without thinking.

"I insist," he repeated. "And as a rule, I have no trouble getting people to obey me."

There was a tense silence between them. Natalie's heart beat fast as she considered his threatening words. Suddenly, though, Ortega seemed to relax. The strange smile he'd given her before reappeared. Natalie recognized it as the smile he'd given her after the accident—a smile that she had found, then, utterly charming.

"Come on," Ortega said pleasantly. "We've talked over all our business. I'd like to call you Ramona and you to call me Marco, as though we were friends."

"We'll never be friends," she replied.

But Ortega seemed determined not to lose his temper.

"What a pity," he said cheerfully. "But for four days at least, I shall indulge my fantasy. Call it what you will. A little luxury . . . a bonus. Can you really object to that, Ramona?"

Natalie couldn't. But nor could she spend four evenings in this man's company.

"Until tomorrow night then, Ramona," Ortega said softly.

"Until tomorrow . . . Marco." Natalie nearly choked on his name. This was going to be the hard part, she suddenly realized. For he really was Marco and somehow just saying his name out loud made her feel strangely closer to him. And that was just what she didn't want.

"You did very well," he teased.

As Marco Ortega turned and walked out of the bar, tossing some bills on the bar as he did so, Natalie couldn't prevent herself from gazing after him. Last night, she thought miserably, she'd stood dreaming about this very man. A man she'd believed to be as honest and kind as he was handsome. And now it was all over.

Chapter 7

Natalie knew that Ramona might be waiting anxiously to hear about her meeting with Ortega so, ignoring her desperate longing to be alone with her thoughts, she stopped off at room 215. She expected, however, that Ramona would be asleep; she would just check in on her. Careful that no one saw her, she slipped her passkey into the lock and quickly entered the suite.

In spite of the sedative that the nurse had given Ramona several hours before, she was awake and restless. Books and magazines were scattered at the side of her bed. Obviously she had attempted to read in order to make the time pass more quickly and had given up impatiently.

"Oh, Natalie, it's you at last!" she cried. "Are you all right? Quick. Come and tell me what happened, I'm dying to know."

For Ramona's sake, Natalie struggled to appear calm. She was upset by the discovery of her feelings for Ortega and close to collapsing from her recent ordeal, but, she reasoned, there was no need to convey this to the excitable Ramona. Briefly she outlined the events of that evening to her.

To her immense relief, Ramona didn't seem to be too concerned by Ortega's demand for the additional one million francs. "Oh well," she shrugged, "I suppose there's nothing we can do. I'm sure Eduardo will have enough money and that's what matters. By the way, I sent a telegram to him this evening. It will be waiting for him when he arrives and I'm sure that he'll send the money immediately."

Then, in an exhausted voice, Natalie explained Ortega's additional conditions. To her surprise and annoyance, Ramona seemed to think that the entire arrangement was funny. Flopping back on her pillows, she laughed uncontrollably.

"Imagine! Four nights with a gangster! And he won't be able to touch you because if anything happens to 'Ramona Martinez,' he won't get his money! Oh, how I would have loved to get a look at him! But of course that's impossible," she said, becoming serious. "Now that you've started this, you will go through with it won't you, Natalie?" Ramona looked at her anxiously.

Natalie was too exhausted to say what was on her mind—that she thought it was all very well for Ramona, safely in bed at the Hotel de Paris, to think that the entire thing was an amusing escapade; for her, though, it was much more disturbing.

"We'll discuss it later," she promised. "If I don't get some sleep soon, I'm going to keel over. Then we'll both be up the creek!"

IT WAS ALMOST NOON before Natalie saw Ramona again. She had managed to catch a few hours of extra sleep and was feeling much better. Since one of the other maids had offered to work her morning shift, she didn't have to start work until two o'clock and had decided to take advantage of the glorious day to enjoy a quick swim. Her swimsuit and towel over her arm, Natalie dropped by to say hello to Ramona.

Ramona's attitude, though, had changed. She seemed frightened and looked anxiously at Natalie for reassurance.

"You will go tonight, won't you, Natalie? Please, don't give up now. All I ask is that you see Ortega and put up with him for the next few evenings. After that, you'll never lay eyes on him again and I promise that you'll never regret what you've done for me."

Embarrassed, Natalie assured Ramona that she would go through with the rest of the ordeal. She suspected that Ramona was willing to pay her, a matter she refused to consider.

"What I'm doing, I'm doing out of friendship, Ramona. Let's leave it at that, all right?"

But Natalie had found it difficult to calm Ramona. She seemed terrified that Ortega might come to the hotel; it had taken all of Natalie's ingenuity to convince her that as long as she remained here at the Hotel de Paris it was unlikely that Ortega would guess he was being deceived.

Now as she walked across the brilliantly lighted square that fronted the public beach she found herself wondering, not for the first time, if friendship really was her only motive. Unable to answer her own question, she put it out of her mind and looked around for Jack, whom she knew, would be eagerly waiting for her.

For once, though, Jack had not been the first to arrive. Unhurried, Natalie changed into her sleek green bathing suit and terry-cloth robe in one of the brightly painted wooden huts that dotted the beach. As she searched for a spot where she could lie in the sun, she felt in the mood to just stretch out on the sand and toast herself. It would be nice for a change just to think about the pleasure of the moment and nothing else.

But just as she was beginning to relax, out of the corner of her eye she spotted Jack's rented Citroën draw up at the curb. He parked and began to walk quickly in her direction; Natalie could tell that he was full of things he wanted to say. With a sigh that she tried to disguise as a smile, she turned to greet him.

"I'm really upset, Natalie," he began, before he had even sat down beside her. "Four lousy days are all I have to spend with you and already you've ruined one night! I'm beginning to wonder if you intend to spend any time with me at all."

Natalie groaned inwardly.

"I hope that you *are* free—" Jack started but Natalie interrupted him and, from the look in his eyes, she knew that he sensed what was coming.

"Jack, I'm so sorry. But it's true, I am busy for the rest of the week and there's nothing I can do to get out of it. I really regret it, but don't forget that you did arrive here unexpectedly."

"Busy . . . with whom?" he demanded.

Natalie paused. She couldn't possibly tell Jack the truth. She could easily imagine him protesting that she was out of her mind to agree to several dates with a blackmailer. And he would argue that she was equally out of her mind to risk her neck for some spoiled, little rich darling who didn't have enough brains to get herself out of a mess she'd got herself into in the first place.

Perhaps, though, she reflected, she should tell Jack about what was going on for her own safety. After all, if Ortega had something else up his sleeve, it would be just as well if Jack knew about it. Then, at least, he would be able to tell the police the entire story. But no, under the circumstances Natalie decided she would have to trust Ramona. What could possibly happen, anyway? It was just a question of waiting a few days more until the money arrived.

Yet the more she thought about it, the more she realized that she was worried that Jack, if he found out, would blow the entire thing apart. If he saw her with Ortega, for instance, he was capable of doing anything out of jealousy. He'd probably apologize later, of course, but by then the damage would have been done. No, this time, she was truly on her own.

"It has to do with my job at the hotel, Jack," she explained patiently. "That's all I can say at the moment. In three days' time—"

"I'll be gone," he finished glumly. Then, without saying another word, he grabbed his towel and started for the beach hut.

A few moments later Jack rejoined her. His expression

was contrite as he settled himself beside her. "I'm doing my best to understand," he said, "but frankly I don't. I guess I'll just have to accept the situation, right?"

Natalie smiled. "Thanks, Jack. I'm sure you won't find Monte Carlo dull without me."

A short while later she made her way back to the hotel, leaving Jack to enjoy the beach. She had work to do. . . .

IT WAS JUST NINE o'clock when Natalie's taxi pulled up in front of the Yachtman. To her surprise Ortega was standing outside the bar, obviously waiting for her. He was at the car before she could open the door.

"Wait," he told her. He leaned over and spoke to the taxi driver through the window. His face, framed by the car window, reminded Natalie sharply of their first meeting and of the effect on her then of his gleaming white teeth, his dark complexion and even darker eyes.

But tonight it was different. She knew who he was now. And they were on a lonely coastal road at sundown. The bar looked deserted, and once the taxi driver had left, she would be alone with this man. A blackmailer . . . a criminal.

Natalie couldn't still the fear rising in her. What a fool she had been to promise to meet him, and here of all places!

"Don't get out of the car," Ortega ordered.

"But—but I'd rather . . ." she stammered. Ortega paid her no attention as he opened the passenger door of the back seat. Nudging her over to make room for himself, he slid in beside her.

"Where are we going?" Natalie asked, frightened.

Ortega leaned forward and closed the glass partition that separated their compartment from the driver's seat. Then he turned and smiled at Natalie.

"What's wrong, Ramona? You look nervous. There's nothing to be afraid of. On the contrary, I'm taking you to the safest place in town. The casino. I can't possibly harm you there."

"Why the casino?" Natalie asked, puzzled and relieved at the same time.

"Oh, no real reason. It just suddenly dawned on me that a woman of your style and habits would prefer a casino to a deserted, run-down coastal bar. And since I know my company is not, er, welcome, I thought you would be able to endure me more comfortably in Monte Carlo."

Natalie couldn't believe her ears. He sounded too smooth, too concerned for her. Something was up.

"I'm not dressed for the casino," she protested, knowing full well this wasn't true. For earlier that evening, she and Ramona had gone through Ramona's extensive wardrobe, choosing the clothes Natalie would wear for the next few evenings. And during the drive out to the bar, Natalie hadn't been able to prevent herself from admiring her reflection in the car window. She had wondered then if she would find it difficult, when all this was over, to return to her own humble wardrobe.

But as Ortega eyed her appreciatively, apparently rejecting her statement, Natalie wished that she had decided to stick with her own simple clothes, instead of giving in to Ramona's enthusiastic recommendations. She was wearing a light pink silk dress with gray stripes, and a beautifully cut gray summer coat. With matching bag and light pink summer shoes, she was dressed perfectly suitably for the casino and they both knew it. Ortega didn't even bother to answer her objections.

"Care for a cigarette?"

"I see that your manners have improved since last night. Have you been practicing?" Natalie knew she was pushing him with her caustic remarks, but she couldn't help it. She felt she was being tricked and resented it.

In what seemed like an impossibly short time, the taxi pulled up outside the casino. Suddenly Natalie understood why Ortega had brought her here. He did suspect her. . . . Why hadn't she realized it at once? What could be more public than the casino? Ramona Martinez was well-known here, and sooner or later during the course of the evening someone would be sure to tell Ortega that the young woman on his arm was not the famous Ramona Martinez but an imposter.

Natalie was thoroughly worried now. She had seen enough of Ortega to guess that he was a mean and vengeful man. Once he found out that he'd been tricked, he would stop at nothing to retaliate. The casino and the square, both of which she'd seen a number of times since coming to Monte Carlo, now seemed unfamiliar and threatening.

"I'm tired," Natalie said, as Ortega put out his hand to help her from the taxi. "What more can you possibly want of me, in any case? I showed up at the Yachtman, as I said I would. Please let me go home, Mr. Ortega."

Ortega didn't answer immediately. He seemed to be debating within himself, although Natalie wasn't sure.

Suddenly he burst out laughing.

"What's all this 'Mr. Ortega' business? I thought we got

that straight last night. We were going to call each other by our first names, or have you forgotten already? You're very young to have such a poor memory, Ramona."

Relieved that he didn't seem to suspect her of not being Ramona Martinez, Natalie fell silent. It was possible that he really did just want to spend some time in the casino, she decided. It was certainly more amusing than the bar and if they didn't stay too long and he didn't introduce her to anyone, it was more than possible that she'd get away with it.

As Ortega held out his arm to her, he spoke in low tones so that the other couples entering the casino with them couldn't hear. "As for your claim to be tired, Ramona, I just don't believe you. First you said that you weren't dressed properly for the casino." Ortega's dark eyes rested on hers in a way that made it clear he found her very attractive. Natalie felt a slow blush spreading over her face. "And we both know that's silly," he added. "But now you are tired. An equally ridiculous excuse. The truth is that you don't enjoy my company. Isn't that so?"

Natalie refused to look at him. But she still hesitated. Why was it so difficult for her to tell this man that she did hate his company? If she did, he might let her return to the hotel and the horrible ordeal awaiting her in the casino could be averted.

"Yes," she finally answered. "I do hate it."

Instantly Ortega's mask was back in place. "Aren't you being a bit standoffish for a girl who owes me one and a half million francs?" he taunted. "I suggest that you save the hard-to-get routine for a man who doesn't have your bad check in his wallet."

Natalie bit back an angry reply. Why had she been reluctant to tell him she hated his company? She did. And she hated him even more at that moment.

Ortega, however, no longer seemed angry. They walked together through the wide swinging doors into the casino, and the pressure of his arm linked through hers was gentle. Natalie didn't dare try to withdraw her hand. She was afraid that he would cause a scene and the most important thing, she reminded herself, was to remain as unobtrusive as possible.

"Well, Ramona," he remarked, "you may not find me exciting company but for my part, I think you're absolutely charming. Whether you detest my presence or not, I insist that you stay here with me until midnight. Then, my lovely Cinderella, you will be free to make your getaway."

But Natalie only half heard him. She was too aware of his closeness, of the pleasant sound of his voice in her ears. She struggled to remain on her guard. For Marco Ortega it was only a game, and he would play it any way that he thought would help him. And if that included pretending he was attracted to her, Natalie was sure that he'd do that, too.

"I know how much you love gambling," he said as he took some money from his wallet and handed it to the cashier. "This isn't a loan, Cinderella, it's a present from me. You don't have to pay me back unless you win. I've heard so much about your gambling from Carlos that I'm curious to see you in action." With an enigmatic smile he handed her the two chips the cashier had given him.

Natalie looked at him, too stunned to say anything. So Ortega did suspect her identity after all. And he was going to test her by seeing how well she handled herself at the tables. Well, in that case, Natalie thought despairingly, the game would soon be up. It would be impossible to convince a man like Ortega that she was an experienced gambler.

"I don't want to play. I hate gambling now," she claimed, hoping Ortega would buy her sudden conversion.

She wasn't surprised to hear his skeptical laugh.

"That's an incredibly quick cure," he commented. "Do you really expect me to believe that this little episode has cured you of gambling once and for all? I am not a fool, Ramona. Once a gambler, always a gambler. And I should know."

It was clear that the only way out was to bluff. Natalie thanked her lucky stars that she'd been in enough amateur theater productions to have at least a basic idea of how to act, for she was about to play the most important role of her short life.

She gave Ortega a cold glance and said, as condescendingly as she could, "I suppose you consider yourself to be an expert on this matter, as on everything else, Mr. Ortega."

"Marco," he said, smiling irritatingly.

"Marco," she repeated. "You obviously have no idea of what I've been going through," she went on haughtily. "It would be enough to end an addiction even greater than mine. But if you insist, I'm perfectly happy to play with your money. I only warn you, I've been on a losing streak for simply ages and you're bound to lose every penny."

They strolled up to a table of thirty or forty people and Natalie found a seat. She looked around at the other players to see what they were doing, at the same time trying to remember how Jack had played the other evening. How she wished she'd paid more attention!

The croupier called out, "Red, odd and manque."

Natalie didn't understand the meanings of the terms and looked around to see what the others were doing. The man next to her left his chips where he'd placed them on the table, so Natalie did the same. She could feel Ortega's presence behind her and shivered slightly.

Her heart almost stopped, though, when the croupier, pointing to her little pile, asked, "Whose chips are those?"

Before she could say anything, Marco replied, "They're *mademoiselle*'s."

The croupier's rake shoved a pile of chips in front of her. Suddenly Natalie realized that she must have won. She thought she could sense Ortega looking at her strangely and knew that he must be aware of how unsure she was. But he just smiled at her and said easily, "Now that you've won, lend me two chips, won't you?"

As she held them out for him, Ortega bent down and, just for an instant, she caught sight of the back of his neck, covered with thick silky hair. He seemed even more handsome and, disconcerted by her reaction, Natalie edged away. How she wished she didn't have to deal with her unfortunate emotions.

Natalie could only hope that Ortega would put down her odd behavior to the excitement caused by gambling. Certainly that would be in keeping with the character of Ramona Martinez. Ortega, however, seemed oblivious.

"Ramona, I'm sorry," he smiled. "I'm afraid that I have been very rude. I can see that you are really tired. I'll take you home soon. Just give me a minute or two to see if I can make a little money and then we'll go. I promise."

"Black, odd and pass," called the croupier.

Marco sighed impatiently. "Well, that's that," he shrugged. "We may as well leave."

Natalie thought he was far too fatalistic about his losses. Surely only a man with money to burn could afford to behave like that. But if he had so much, why did he want more? Or was that the way he got his money in the first place—from victims like Ramona Martinez? Natalie shuddered in distaste.

"It really doesn't matter, you know," Ortega said, turning to her, almost as if he had read her thoughts. "After all, how could I expect Lady Luck to smile on me when I've already got more than my fair share—with the prettiest girl in Monte Carlo at my side? I'm not a greedy man. I'm happy with what I've got." He laughed, taking her arm again. Relaxed, he was gazing at Natalie with a look that was so tender, so enveloping that she thought she might drown in the depths of his dark eyes.

Afraid once again that her feelings would overwhelm her better judgment, Natalie tore her eyes away from Marco's tender gaze and walked along toward the casino exit. As she did so, the light silk scarf she had been wearing loosely tied around her neck floated to the floor. Natalie, however, didn't notice it was missing. Marco picked it up and slipped it into his jacket pocket.

"I want to thank you for letting me leave," Natalie said as Ortega joined her on the steps outside the casino. "It's not necessary for you to take me back to the hotel. I can find my way from here."

"Of course you can, my little Cinderella," he teased. "But it's not yet midnight and I have the pleasure of your company until then. So, I plan to escort you back to the hotel, whether you like it or not."

But before they'd reached the bottom of the casino steps, a young red-haired woman dressed in a skimpy jade green evening dress with a black mink stole thrown carelessly over her shoulders, called out to Ortega. She was just getting out of an enormous white Cadillac and Natalie saw her first. She fell back a step and Ortega, obviously recognizing the young woman, ran forward to greet her.

"Maria! How nice to see you. And what a surprise! I thought you were still in Paris."

"Well, as you can see, I'm not," came the laughing reply. "And who is this lovely young lady?" Maria asked, examining Natalie carefully while she kissed Marco on the cheek.

"This is Ramona Martinez, Arturo Martinez's daughter. Your fathers have been friends since childhood. I thought you knew each other."

"I . . . I don't believe we have met," Natalie said in a low voice, certain she was about to be unmasked.

To her astonishment, though, Maria said indifferently, "Oh, no, we haven't met. I'm a few years older than Ramona and somehow we were never in the same place at the same time."

Seeing that Natalie seemed anxious, and mistaking it for a desire to leave the casino, Maria added, "Please, don't let me detain you. Shall we meet tomorrow for lunch, *querido*?"

"Why yes, let's," Ortega said easily. He kissed her hand

with an old-world grace that Natalie found charming. "We can catch up on gossip and other matters then."

"Done!" Maria blew a kiss in Natalie's direction and sauntered into the casino.

Once again Marco slipped his arm through Natalie's and they began to stroll in the direction of the Hotel de Paris.

"Maria's an old friend of mine," he explained. "We both grew up in Spain. I wasn't always a criminal, you know, Ramona. I am the son of a well-known and highly respectable Spanish family. We go back to the fourteenth century."

Suddenly the blood slowed in Natalie's veins.

"You grew up in Madrid?" she asked in a small voice. Ortega must have met the real Ramona, she thought in terror.

"Oh, no," Marco's reply was offhanded. "Had I grown up there, I would have met you at one point. And if I had," he added gently, "I would never have forgotten your face."

They walked slowly along the sidewalk that led to the hotel. Soon Natalie could see the window of her room. They stopped and stood near the lamppost where Carlos and Ramona had had their quarrel only two nights earlier. To Natalie, standing there confused and uncertain, it seemed that years had passed since then.

As they turned to the elaborately landscaped patio and stairs leading to the hotel entrance, Natalie put out her hand. "I'll leave you here," she said as firmly as she could, hoping that Ortega wouldn't protest.

But he did. "What's the matter, Ramona? Are you ashamed to be seen with me? You must have plenty of gentlemen friends. As far as the hotel employees and other guests are concerned, I'll just be one more. Or am I not presentable enough?" he asked, imitating her earlier excuse.

They both knew that this was far from being the case; if Natalie hadn't been so nervous about being seen with Ortega, she would have smiled. As a hotel employee, though, she was supposed to enter and leave from the side door.

"You can come in with me, if you insist," she said reluctantly. After all, it wasn't that important. Even if the desk clerk, Dominique, did notice, he would just assume that she'd been out on a date and had decided it was late enough to come in through the front entrance. She was pretty sure that he wasn't the type to gossip.

"Good," Marco said. "It doesn't worry me in the least." And he gave an odd little laugh.

As it turned out, Dominique wasn't at his desk and the lobby was deserted.

"Well, are you satisfied now?" Natalie asked, turning to Marco. "There's no one here to show how presentable you are, so why don't you leave?"

"I'm going," came the even reply, "but not until I see you safely to the elevator."

"Oh, I usually take the stairs," she said quickly. Natalie had no wish to confront the elevator operator at this time of night. He was an old gossip and she didn't trust him at all.

"Good night, then, Cinderella. I'll see you tomorrow. Don't forget."

Ortega stood watching Natalie as she wandered toward the stairs and when she turned to see if he was still there, he gave her a friendly wave. To any onlookers, Natalie thought as she mounted the stairs, their parting would have seemed like the normal farewell of a couple who had just spent a very pleasant evening together.

When she'd reached the landing on the second floor, a strong breeze blew at her from the open window down the hall. She shivered and instinctively her hand went up to tighten the silk scarf. The last thing she needed right now was to catch a cold. She was surprised and disconcerted to find it gone. Ramona would be upset if she had lost it. It had been a gift from her brother, Eduardo, and Ramona had insisted that Natalie wear it for good luck.

Wondering if perhaps she'd dropped it during her hasty flight up the stairs, Natalie carefully retraced her steps. But there was no scarf. Ortega would have left the lobby by now she was sure, so she decided to check there just in case she had dropped it on her way in. Tomorrow, if necessary, she would go to the casino and see if anyone had picked it up; perhaps it had been left there with the management. She stiffened in distaste at the idea.

To Natalie's surprise, as she rounded the stairs, she could see Ortega still standing in the foyer. She drew back quickly, certain that he hadn't seen her. Luckily for her, he had been looking the other way.

Dominique must have returned to his desk at the same time as Natalie spotted Ortega, for the clerk walked over to Ortega and looked questioningly at him. Ortega realized that he was going to be asked to account for his presence in the lobby. Natalie watched as he reached into his pocket and handed Ramona's scarf to Dominique.

"Would you be good enough to return this scarf to Miss Martinez?" Ortega asked politely. "She asked me to keep it for her."

The liar. What was he up to, Natalie wondered. She leaned forward to get a better view of what was going on. With a gasp she felt her balance going and only just managed to avoid slipping and falling down the remaining stairs—probably to land with a bump in full view of Dominique and Marco.

Her balance restored, if not her dignity, Natalie's nervousness changed to terror. Of course Dominique would know that Ramona was ill in bed. He would wonder what was going on and might even give their secret away.

He did know it, in fact. Natalie could tell by the cautious way in which he spoke to Ortega.

"*Monsieur* says he went out this evening with Mademoiselle Martinez?" he repeated slowly, and to Natalie's ear at least, skeptically.

Ortega was annoyed. He obviously felt that the desk clerk was being impertinent.

"Do you see anything wrong with that?" he said, looking hard at Dominique.

Dominique averted his eyes and adopted a more respectful tone.

"Forgive me, *monsieur*. I thought that . . . Miss Martinez was very tired."

Natalie held her breath. So far, Dominique was being very discreet. But still, he had said something that Marco could check out, if he was in the least suspicious. He could easily discover that Ramona had, in fact, spent the entire evening in bed. But for some reason, Ortega seemed to take the clerk's information quite calmly.

"Well, I don't know what you're so upset about. I'm quite aware that Miss Martinez was tired. In fact, she asked me to bring her back to the hotel early so that she could get

.

a good night's rest. Now, would you be good enough to deliver that scarf to her room?" Ortega turned on his heels and swiftly left the hotel.

Natalie waited until she was sure that Ortega would be some distance away from the hotel. She had decided to take the scarf up to Ramona's room herself. That way she hoped to put an end to the entire incident.

"Ah, it's you, Mademoiselle Davis," Dominique said amiably as she walked casually into the lobby. "It's late for you to be up. You're on the early shift these days, aren't you?"

"Yes, I am," she replied, coming up to the desk. She perched on it in a friendly manner. "I couldn't sleep so I decided to take a walk."

"Oh, I don't know that it's all that safe for you to go out walking this late at night," Dominique said cautiously.

Grateful for a way out, for she really only wanted to go to bed, Natalie gave the impression that she was thinking his comment over. Then she smiled.

"You know, I think you're right, Dominique. It *is* a bit late. Maybe I'll just go and check on Miss Martinez instead."

The clerk reacted on cue.

"In that case, Miss Davis," he said, reaching under the counter, "perhaps you would be so kind as to take this up to her. A gentleman was just by. He said that she left it with him earlier this evening. He was quite forceful about the matter and seemed anxious that she get it tonight."

"Of course, I'll take it up to her, Dominique. You shouldn't really leave the desk unattended, should you?" she asked . . . rather too enthusiastically, she thought, although Dominique didn't notice.

With a sigh of relief, Natalie climbed the stairs a second time. Aware that she had been extremely lucky, in this instance, she couldn't help wondering how much longer she could go on playing this dangerous game and winning.

Chapter 8

At first Ramona had been horrified by Natalie's account of her evening with Ortega. She was particularly upset by the episode concerning her scarf. While she was calming Ramona down, Natalie found that her own fears were lessening. Obviously Ortega was not suspicious of her—at least not suspicious enough to try and do anything about it.

"How are you feeling?" Natalie asked in an effort to changed the subject.

"Terrible," Ramona said miserably. "My head aches and I'm so dizzy that I can't walk without feeling like I'm going to fall over."

Natalie was convinced that Ramona's illness was due to nerves, and possibly to a healthy desire to appear as sick as possible so that she wouldn't have to meet Ortega. Natalie smiled. She really couldn't blame Ramona.

"The nurse seems to think you're doing fine. I passed her on my way to your suite just now," Natalie said casually, curious to see how Ramona would react.

"Oh, her! She just wants to keep busy."

"Why don't you come with me for a walk tomorrow, Ramona? I think that some fresh air would do you good. You've been cooped up in here too long."

"I can't," Ramona cried. "What if Ortega, or any of his friends, saw me?"

Natalie decided not to point out that it was highly unlikely that Ramona would run into Ortega. Still, Ramona probably was right. But she wasn't sure whether Ramona's fear was genuine. Was she really all that afraid of Ortega? Perhaps there was something she hadn't mentioned? Natalie felt ashamed of herself for questioning her friend, yet sometimes Ramona's reactions to things puzzled her. At one moment she was like a little girl, happily planning Natalie's wardrobe for her dates with Ortega, completely capable of ignoring the fact that these dates were with a dangerous blackmailer. Then, at the next moment and for no apparent reason, she was utterly terrified and completely dependent on Natalie for advice and instructions. To Natalie, her moods made no sense.

Unable to calm Ramona any more than she had already done, Natalie said good-night. As she thought about the evening to come, she felt her heartbeat quicken. Was it possible that she was actually looking forward to her evenings with Ortega? Quickly she banished the thought from her mind. She couldn't afford to look forward to seeing him, or to anything that had to do with him. He was her enemy, she reminded herself fiercely until she fell into an exhausted sleep.

NATALIE'S MORNING SWIM with Jack was uneventful. But at least, she noticed gratefully, he showed signs of believing that her evenings really were tied up, and not with another

man. How ironic, Natalie reflected; just as it was no longer
the case, Jack was beginning to believe her. For Marco
Ortega was in her thoughts constantly. She found it impossible not to think of him and it frightened her. She'd
never felt this way about anyone before and the last person
in the world she wished to think about was Ortega.

"I've managed to wangle another forty-eight hours in
Monte Carlo," Jack told her happily. "And I plan to spend
all of them with you."

Again Natalie wondered if she was being fair. Perhaps
she should tell Jack, in terms that even he wouldn't be able
to misunderstand, that he was wasting his time with her?
But right now, when she was so in need of a friend, even if
he didn't actually know what was going on, she found it
difficult to do. Even if it was for his own good. And even if
she was being selfish.

Natalie sighed. Jack, who was lying on the sand beside
her, mistook her sigh for one of disappointment.

"Does that displease you so much, Lili?" he asked in hurt
tones.

"Of course not," she said hastily. "In fact, I was thinking
of something else. I'll be happy to spend some time with
you when all this is over."

At about seven o'clock, Natalie decided to skip dinner with
the other maids and, instead, lie down for two hours. But
as she lay on her bed trying to relax, she was filled with a
strange feeling of excitement. And yet her excitement was
mixed with a feeling of lassitude.

She wondered if it might be the fresh, balmy Mediterranean air that left her feeling so dreamy and open to
physical sensation. She could imagine feeling this way if
she'd met some devastatingly attractive man who'd come

into her dull life at the Hotel de Paris and, falling madly in love with her, had swept her off her feet. But to feel this way about Marco Ortega! He was a blackmailer, a cheat, she told herself for the hundredth time. And for all she knew, he might even be a murderer as well.

Only a few weeks earlier she had been living the hardworking, uneventful life of a student in Paris. Now she was working in a city that had been called a sunny place for shady people. And she was involved with an heiress and a blackmailer. Well, she reminded herself reluctantly, it had been in the hope of finding adventure and romance that she had decided to come to Monte Carlo. She had certainly found more than she had bargained for and just hoped that it didn't turn out to be more than she could handle.

As she lay there she wondered about what she should wear that evening. Unconsciously she echoed Ramona's words. "I must look my best tonight."

But somehow, Natalie found it almost impossible to get up. Ortega's face appeared in her mind and she traced the strong lines of his chin with her fingers, remembering the thick black curls at the back of his neck and the way he had of caressing her with his eyes. As the sweet smell of mimosa and oleander filled her room, she closed her eyes and imagined what it might have been like if only Ortega had been the man of her dreams and not a criminal. . . .

Her daydream was broken by the telephone's sharp ring.

"Natalie!" It was Ramona's voice. Natalie barely recognized it. "Please come. Quickly!"

Before Natalie could ask her what was wrong, Ramona had hung up. Obviously someone else was with her, or she had been too upset to talk. Was it possible—Natalie was panic-stricken—that Ortega had found the real Ramona and was with her now?

Natalie rushed to Ramona's room and breathlessly entered. A glance told her that her worst fears were unfounded. Ortega wasn't there.

"What is it?" Natalie asked, on the point of anger.

Shaking with sobs, Ramona pointed to a letter that lay in front of her on the bed. "I'm sorry, Natalie," she said in a choked voice. "It's just that I'm so frightened. It's a letter from Carlos and it's hateful! He tells me how much he loved me, how much I meant to him, until I had to go and ruin it all with my gambling. He says that I killed his love for me, that he's glad Ortega has the check because he'll teach me a lesson. . . ."

Natalie found it difficult to believe that anyone, let alone a man who claimed to love her, could be so cruel to Ramona. Surely they saw in her what she saw—a beautiful and charming but very spoiled and selfish young woman, who was also kind and naive. Ramona needed looking after; she just wasn't capable of looking after herself. Natalie had already decided that when all this was over she would write to Mr. Martinez herself and, tactfully of course, tell him that his daughter was in need of more guidance and advice from her father than he perhaps realized.

"He despises me!" Ramona cried, the tears still streaming down her face. Natalie had never seen her so upset.

"Oh, I know I did something terribly wrong. I can even understand how he feels. But he said he loved me before and I believed him! If he loved me, how could he do this to me?" she asked pathetically.

"What Carlos did was wrong, Ramona," Natalie said

firmly. "He's treated you very badly. And he's been cowardly as well. If he had to deal with your brother, or your father, he would have behaved differently. No, to bring in an unscrupulous blackmailer like Ortega is a coward's act."

"That's what I think, too." Ramona said, brightening a little. It crossed Natalie's mind that Ramona was so innocent that it was just possible she would accept the opinion of anyone—if she liked him enough. The thought made Natalie shudder and hope, for everybody's sake, that Ramona never fell into the hands of unscrupulous people. But hadn't she? And hadn't someone taken pity on her?

"I don't know if he's always like this," Natalie continued. "I suppose one would have to know him longer to find out. But if his revenge is motivated only by the fact that you signed a bad check, I'd say that he never really loved you in the first place."

Ramona nodded. "If he had really loved me, he would have forgiven me."

Natalie looked at her. "I think so."

"It's crazy, I know," Ramona said slowly, looking at Natalie with tear-filled eyes, "but I . . ."

". . . Still love him?" Natalie volunteered.

"Yes," Ramona said quickly. "Do you think I'm crazy?"

"Not at all, Ramona," Natalie said affectionately. "You're not alone." And suddenly she realized that she'd openly admitted what she'd known for some time: that she, like Ramona, loved a man in spite of what he was was. Ortega! She loved him, in spite of the fact that he was a notorious blackmailer who would stop at nothing to get what he wanted.

She knew she should hate him, but she had tried to and

couldn't. Ashamed of herself for being so weak—after all, Ramona was inexperienced and naive but she, Natalie Davis, should know better—Natalie vowed that she would keep her feelings to herself. Ortega would never know.

When the telephone rang, Natalie automatically reached to answer it. She had been in this room so often during the past few days that she almost felt if she was in her own room.

"Hello," she said politely.

"Hello. It's me," a man's voice answered. Natalie knew instantly that it was Ortega and thanked whoever it was who was watching over her that it had been she and not Ramona, who'd picked up the receiver. "Do you know who this is?"

"Of course." Natalie was annoyed. With the telephone between her and Ortega she felt quite daring. "Were you afraid that I'd skipped town? No, you panicked and read the clock wrong, is that it? Don't worry, I'll be there as we arranged."

Natalie was suddenly nervous when there was no answer at the other end. "I'm sorry," she stammered into the phone, unaware that Ramona had stopped sobbing and was listening intently. "I shouldn't have said those things. But why are you calling? Do you want to meet somewhere else?"

Ortega's abrupt laugh sounded ominous on the telephone.

"Not at all, my dear little Ramona. It's simply that I have better things to do tonight than meet you. I've seen you once already today. This morning, down on the beach with your young friend. I'm certain, you see, that you're in town and should like, if you'll permit me, to reclaim my freedom for this evening and give you back yours. I'm sure, too, that you'll be delighted to have the evening to yourself. I can't say that I'm sorry, either. We'll see each other tomorrow night. It will be our last night. The end of your agony and of my patience. Meanwhile, enjoy yourself." Ortega hung up before Natalie had a chance to respond.

Ramona was silently eyeing her. Natalie was clearly angry.

"That brute!" Natalie cried. "It's not enough that he terrorizes us with his vicious threats of blackmail. He thinks that he can just make a fool of anyone he likes. Who does he think he is? When I've got you out of this mess, Ramona, we'll just see who is Mr. Irresistible!"

Unable to keep back the tears, but no longer caring that Ramona should see her so upset, she continued, "Yes, dear Mr. Ortega, you've given me my freedom for the evening and I intend to make the most of it, I can assure you."

Natalie stormed out of the room, leaving a startled and puzzled Ramona to fit the pieces together as best as she could.

JACK WAS DELIGHTED when Natalie phoned to tell him that she was free to go out with him now.

"I'll be right over," he said happily. "It's high time we went to the casino and blew that money I won the other night."

"No, Jack." Natalie said, in a voice that was unusually tender. "If you don't mind too much, I'd rather go dancing with you at the Sea Club."

"That's the place where they have dancing under the stars, isn't it?"

"Yes, and a great orchestra."

"Terrific. The sea, the night, music and you! What more could a guy want?"

Natalie refused to listen to her conscience as she got ready to meet Jack. She put on one of her own dresses, a particularly nice one of rich emerald green that clung to her slender body and emphasized her delicate lines. It was Jack's favorite.

But they couldn't have been at the Sea Club for more than twenty minutes before Natalie knew she wouldn't be able to stand it. Ortega was constantly in her thoughts and she had to fight to keep the tears of frustration and disappointment from her eyes. She was furious with herself but it didn't seem to make any difference. Perhaps, she concluded, the best thing to do would be to go to bed and try to forget her misery in sleep.

"What's the matter, Lili?" Jack asked.

I'd better get out of here, she thought, *before I end up alienating the one person in the world who really seems to care for me.*

"Let's go. You were right, Jack. We should have gone to the casino instead."

Good-natured as ever, Jack followed her without a word. But Natalie knew from his silence that he was deeply puzzled by her behavior. In order to get to the door they had to thread their way through a group of tables that had been crowded together to make room for some unexpected guests. To her horror Natalie found herself walking directly toward a table occupied by an attractive young couple. An extremely pretty redhead, exotically dressed in a low-necked evening gown, was leaning intimately across the table toward her dark-haired companion. It was Marco

Ortega and Maria, the woman Natalie had met the night before.

She swerved sharply, almost knocking a glass of wine off the adjacent table. The man to whom the glass belonged seemed about to make some remark, but when he saw Natalie's face, he quickly turned back to his companions.

"But what . . ." Jack began, hurrying to keep up with her.

"But . . . what?" the red-faced Natalie snapped back, unable to check her anger.

"Isn't that the guy we saw in the white car the other night?"

"It is, indeed," she ground out.

But Ortega had seen them and was signaling to Jack to come over to their table. Suddenly Jack put out his arm and stopped her. Now along with her fury at Ortega Natalie was faced with the possibility that Jack might unwittingly betray her.

"Please, let's get out of here," she begged.

Jack heard the note of desperation in her voice and waved at Ortega, indicating that they were in a hurry. But as soon as they had reached the steps he turned and stared at Natalie in amazement.

"For God's sake, what's the matter with you?" he demanded. "I've known you for years and I've never seen you behave like that. And tonight's not the only time. You've changed since you've come to Monte Carlo."

Jack said nothing more and went to get the Citroën. But Natalie knew what he had meant to say—only was too polite, too loyal—was that he didn't like the change very much.

Chapter 9

The next morning, after their swim together, Natalie apologized to Jack for her behavior the previous evening.

"I'm really sorry, Jack. I'm just caught up in something at work and it's affecting me in ways that I can't tell you about. At least not yet."

As she spoke, Natalie blushed, for she knew perfectly well that it had been jealousy that had caused her behavior. But Jack had accepted her apology with his usual good humor. He had already forgotten the entire incident, he told her a little uncertainly.

Natalie decided to take the bus back to the hotel since Jack seemed reluctant to leave the beach. In spite of herself her thoughts turned to Ortega and the matter of getting Ramona's check back. The check was Ortega's carte blanche to treat her just as he liked, and she wished desperately that she could just forget him.

But she comforted herself with the idea that even if she

hadn't been able to help falling in love with him, she would never have considered marriage to such a man. Respect, she knew, was the most important ingredient in any successful marriage and she could never deeply respect a man like Ortega—however much she was attracted to him. She and Ramona had agreed on that, as they had agreed on many things. Gradually, as Natalie got to know the Spanish girl better, she'd found herself liking her more and more. For in spite of their many differences, they seemed to look at life—and particularly love—in the same way.

As the bus neared the casino square, Natalie thought about the work she knew would be piled high, waiting for her. She got off and hurried around the corner to the hotel. Abruptly someone stepped onto the path directly in front of her. Because the sun was in her eyes and she'd forgotten to wear her sunglasses, it took Natalie a few seconds to recognize who it was. *Ortega.* Her heart began to pound.

"I'm very glad to see you," he said, smiling.

As she looked at him, Natalie knew it would be hard to find a more elegant young man in all Monte Carlo. He wore a V-necked white shirt and white trousers that fitted his slim hips to perfection. But why did he have to turn up now, she thought despairingly, when she was trying so hard not to think of him.

"The least you could say is that you're happy to see me as well," Ortega remarked. "Though I wouldn't believe you, anyway," he added laughingly. "But surely you're smart enough to realize that it would be in your best interests to at least pretend you're glad to see me, if that's what I want?"

"I'm not a hypocrite," Natalie flung at him. Then she

remembered Jack and wondered if she had a right to make such a claim.

"Our relationship is strictly business and I plan to keep it that way," she said more calmly.

But when Ortega looked hard into Natalie's eyes she had to turn her head. She couldn't afford to let him see the least emotion in her expression. There was no telling how he'd use the knowledge that she was attracted to him.

"Excuse me, but I'm expected at the hotel," she said, longing for the sanctuary of the hotel.

"I'll walk up with you," he offered. He took her arm, apparently aware that there was nothing she could do to stop him. She tried walking quickly, in order to get rid of that disconcerting pressure of his arm on hers.

"Who's expecting you? Jack?"

"Oh, no. I just left him a few minutes ago."

"Ah, yes. The daily session at the beach."

Natalie didn't answer but she glanced at Ortega out of the corner of her eye. He seemed displeased.

Suddenly he turned and stopped her. "Ramona, look at me. Why did you leave the Sea Club the minute you laid eyes on me? I was looking forward to having at least one dance with you."

"Am I not permitted any sort of private life at all?" she inquired. "Do I have to have reasons that satisfy you, that explain everything that I do? Besides, it's none of your business," she ended passionately, desperately hoping he would mistake the unhappiness in her voice for anger.

For a moment Ortega's touch on her arm was tender and he seemed to be considering what she'd said. Would this man never stop surprising her, she wondered. When she expected him to be angry he was tender and, equally suddenly, his gentleness could turn to scorn. She could feel her head beginning to ache and she thought regretfully of the long hot working day ahead of her.

But as far as Ortega was concerned, she was Ramona Martinez, wealthy and spoiled. He probably thought she would spend the rest of the day shopping in the luxury stores of Monte Carlo or eating exquisite little ice creams in an outdoor café, gossiping with her friends. Little did he know . . . . Suddenly Natalie felt sorry for herself. Afraid that Ortega would see the tears beginning to form in her eyes, she jerked away from him. Immediately his mood changed. He looked at her sharply, almost cruelly.

"Just remember this, Ramona: I'm not a man who accepts defeat. In even the smallest things."

"You couldn't have danced with me, anyway. You already had a partner, remember?"

Ortega smiled. He was obviously remembering Maria and their evening together with pleasure.

"She's very pretty, don't you think?"

"Yes, very." Natalie's throat constricted as she spoke.

"She's a friend. An old friend."

"Not so very old," Natalie replied.

Ortega's expression was puzzled. Then he threw back his head and laughed wholeheartedly. He took Natalie's hand and kissed it.

"Thank you!" he said simply.

Natalie tried to protest but he laid a finger gently on her lips.

"No, don't add a word. You've just said the one thing I wanted to hear. By the way," he continued, suddenly becoming businesslike, "how is our little deal coming along? Have you heard from your brother?"

Startled by this abrupt change in the conversation, Natalie could say nothing.

Ortega looked at her calculatingly. "Well?" he drawled, as he lighted a cigarette.

"I expect to hear from my brother today," she said nervously.

"Good." Ortega turned to go. "And you should know that you can thank my attractive young friend for your freedom from the terrible ordeal of spending an evening with me. Now that I've seen you and been reassured that you're not planning to leave Monte Carlo before tomorrow, it won't be necessary for us to meet later on."

Before a shocked Natalie could utter a word, Ortega gave her a friendly wave and walked jauntily down the path.

IT WAS FOUR O'CLOCK that afternoon before Natalie was able to take a break and visit Ramona. She found her sitting on the sun-drenched balcony, idly flipping through some fashion magazines. Dressed in a skimpy bikini, she looked full of life and youthful beauty. Natalie couldn't help thinking at that moment that Ramona was decidedly the healthier of the two of them. It had been a long hot day and she felt drained after working in the steaming laundry and linen room.

Natalie smiled and Ramona turned to her with an expression that was a mixture of pleasure and fear.

"I'm so glad you've come, Natalie. I didn't want to ring the linen room in case I got you into trouble again. But I've wanted to speak to you desperately all day. Look what I received this morning." She flipped a page from the magazine she'd been reading, then held out a slip of paper.

It was a telegram. Natalie knew even before she read it that something had gone wrong. Eduardo's money would not be in Monte Carlo by the next evening.

Natalie looked up as she finished reading the brief message. "But if Eduardo isn't registered as a guest at the Berlin Hilton, then where is he?" she demanded.

"I don't know. Eduardo never stays anywhere else when he's in Berlin. He must have changed his mind, you see, because he always books ahead. Oh, I don't know what to do! My father probably knows where he is, but I'm scared to call him. He would suspect something since I seldom see or write to Eduardo unless it's to ask for money."

It was becoming more and more clear to Natalie from everything that Ramona's troublesome habits had a long history. Was she even sure that she could trust this young woman? That question was always in the back of Natalie's mind and when she least wanted it to surface, it did.

"I'm so frightened," Ramona cried, turning to her. "If Eduardo's money doesn't come by tomorrow evening— and I'm sure now that it won't—I will have to go and tell Ortega myself the whole story. You've taken all the risks up to now, but it would be dishonorable of me not to do this personally. If Ortega becomes desperate," and Ramona's voice quavered, "it's only right that he should know the real Ramona Martinez."

Touched, Natalie could see that Ramona was making an heroic effort to assume responsibility. It seemed that the appalling situation she'd created had taught her a lesson, and Natalie was glad. If only they could give Ortega his money, she was convinced Ramona would be cured of her mania for gambling forever.

"Listen, Ramona: don't do anything rash. We've got to think this through carefully. It would be stupid to tell Ortega everything if he can be convinced to wait a few extra days."

Ramona's face was glowing with hope. "Do you really think it's possible?"

"I don't know," Natalie said, thinking of Ortega's extreme moods. If she asked him at the right moment, she knew that he would give her—them—the extra time they needed to find Eduardo. But if she was unlucky enough to ask him at the wrong time, she was just as certain he would vehemently deny the request. And just what he would do then, Natalie dared not imagine.

"Ramona," she said slowly, "is it possible that Eduardo will be contacting you in any case?"

"It's possible, but I'm never sure. He usually tells me where he is. And I haven't heard from him for some time."

"Well, we've still got until tomorrow," Natalie said, as cheerfully as she could. "Perhaps by then we'll have heard from Eduardo. Or maybe we'll have come up with some great excuse that's bound to convince Ortega to give us the extra time."

Ramona nodded and looked at her unhappily. Suddenly Natalie desperately wanted to get away from her, from the hotel, from everything that reminded her of the one man in the world she wanted to forget. But most of all she wanted to escape from the uncomfortable feeling that she really welcomed this delay, that this was the reason why she felt calm in the face of a situation that only a few days before would have unnerved her. The delay, after all, would mean a few more evenings with Ortega and, she reasoned, since once all this was over she would never—could never—see him again, surely she could see Ramona through this last hurdle.

Natalie excused herself and went up to her room to make a phone call.

For half an hour Natalie and Jack had been sitting in a small coffee house, deciding what to do with the rest of the evening. Jack looked at her closely. "You're not even listening to me, Lili," he complained.

Natalie gave him a tired smile. "I have a headache, that's all. Nothing serious. Would you order me another cup of espresso, please? I need a pick-me-up."

Jack did as she requested, then turned to her with an eager expression on his face.

"I have a surprise for you," he said playfully.

"Oh." Even to Natalie her voice sounded utterly unenthusiastic. In her present mood, the last thing she wanted was a surprise.

"Aren't you even going to ask me what it is?" Jack was taken aback.

"I'm sorry, Jack. What is it?"

"You remember the chap who was so concerned about you the night of the accident?"

"Which one?" she said cautiously.

"Oh, come on, Natalie, surely you haven't forgotten already! We saw him again last night, at the Sea Club. Well, he's meeting us here in about twenty minutes. His name's Ortega." Jack finished, glancing at his watch.

"Where did you meet him?" she asked, her heart pounding.

"On the beach, after you left this morning. I was just getting ready to leave when he came up to me and started asking about you. He was polite and discreet and all that, but I could tell that he's interested in you."

"So what did you do?"

"I told him what he wanted to know. That we weren't engaged." Jack grinned.

"He asked you *that*?" Natalie cried.

"Well, not in so many words. But I knew what he was hinting at, so I decided to put him out of his misery. Shouldn't I have?" Jack looked at Natalie with something like hope in his eyes.

"No. No, of course you should have," Natalie said impatiently. "But how did you end up arranging to meet here?"

"Remember the pretty redhead who was with him at the casino? She's quite something. She was with Marco at the beach, too. Her bikini is even tinier than—"

"Jack!" Natalie wailed.

"Oh, all right," he laughed. "Well she—her name's Maria, actually—she suggested we get together and he gave me a telephone number. Unfortunately Maria couldn't come this evening."

Natalie was confused. Had Jack given away who she really was, or had Ortega somehow managed to remain ignorant of her identity? But she knew that she couldn't rely on Jack to tell her what had happened. He couldn't possibly know whether Ortega had guessed or not.

"So you see, Lili, as soon as I got your message I called Ortega and set up this date. You've been so distant lately, I thought maybe you were a bit bored with me and that you'd enjoy meeting new people."

But Natalie was barely listening. She was trying to figure

out Ortega's motives. Should she stay or try to make Jack leave? But how? It was vital that whatever she did the three of them didn't come together.

She began to fear that Ortega already knew the truth about her and had set up this meeting with the sole purpose of unmasking her. Perhaps he had Ramona at this very moment and was going to confront both of them with their deception? She took a deep breath. She had to keep her head, she reminded herself; the only thing she could do now was hope that Jack hadn't already given her away and get rid of him before Ortega's arrival.

Natalie began to rub her eyes, then turned to Jack, saying, "Maybe I should just go back to the hotel. I've got the most splitting headache."

"I've lost too many of my evenings in Monte Carlo with you already. How about if I went to a drugstore for some aspirin? I won't be long. Besides, I'm sure Ortega will be happy to keep you company alone for a few minutes."

Natalie's heart sank. Her ploy hadn't worked. Jack was pushing her at Ortega! What on earth had got into him, she wondered as Jack hurried away to find a drugstore.

"Good evening, Ramona," a familiar voice said softly.

Natalie looked up in surprise. Mocking as ever, Ortega stood before her. He and Jack must have just missed each other, she thought in relief.

"Where is Jack? Really, I'm disappointed. You make such a nice couple."

"Jack's not feeling well. He wasn't able to come."

"Really? But I saw him go down the street as I drove up." His voice was hard.

"Oh, I sent him to the drugstore to get some aspirin. I told him I had a headache."

"You don't?"

"No, I wanted to see you alone. Let's get out of here."

Ortega nodded.

"You go first," Natalie ordered. "I don't want anyone to see us leaving together."

"The car's parked around the side. I'll meet you there."

After Ortega had left, Natalie quickly scribbled a note for Jack, telling him that she'd gone back to the hotel and asking him to give her apologies to Ortega. The waiter promised to make sure that he received it.

Ortega was at the wheel of his sports car by the time Natalie arrived. He leaned over and opened the door on the passenger side for her. Natalie hesitated in sudden fear.

"Oh, come on, Ramona." Marco snapped his fingers impatiently. "I'm not about to bring the entire Spanish police force down on my head by kidnapping the daughter of one of its most famous citizens. I'm content to wait until tomorrow and take my money and run," he ended sarcastically. "And besides, who's to say that I'm not the one who should be frightened?"

"*You?*" Natalie looked at him quickly. "What do you mean?"

"Well, how do I know that you're not armed? Maybe *you're* desperate enough to force me to return the check. I've heard that you resorted to similar, although less effective means, with Carlos."

Natalie was speechless.

"Consider, after all. Wouldn't it strike you as strange if a woman who claimed my presence was hateful to her suddenly wanted to be alone with me? It's obvious that you engineered that little episode to dispense of Jack. And yet now that we are together you're acting as if you're afraid."

"Oh, let's drive," Natalie snapped.

But Ortega was obviously determined to continue their conversation. Soon he drew up along a quiet stretch of beach separated by a few hundred yards from the shore road.

"If I threaten you at all," he began, "you can simply run to the roadway. Cars are passing by constantly and no one is going to refuse a pretty maiden in distress. Fair enough?"

Natalie nodded.

"And now, Ramona, tell me the truth. What's going on?"

So he did know, Natalie thought in alarm. And now she was alone with him. . . .

"What do you mean?" she said a little unsteadily.

"Have you got the money?"

Natalie tried to keep the relief out of her voice. "No, not yet, but it's on the way."

"You've heard from your brother?" Marco asked in a rather odd voice. Without waiting for her reply, he continued, "Well, no matter. As long as the money's on its way, that's all I care about. After tomorrow, you'll be rid of me forever. You may think that rather peculiar, Ramona, but it's proof that there's some honor among thieves."

Suddenly Ortega laughed and leaned toward her. He took her chin in his hand, turning her toward him. She knew her face was visible in the reflection of the lights that lined the shore road, and Natalie could see Ortega clearly, his dark hair, his fierce eyes almost glowing with intensity in the half-light.

"Just as I thought, Ramona," he said gently. "You look

very unhappy. But you should be happy now that you've heard from your brother."

"I've got a headache," she protested feebly, terribly conscious of the light touch of his hand on her chin, his body inches from hers. But he didn't let her go. Instead his eyes pierced hers in the darkness.

"And now I'm going to tell you the truth. . . ."

Natalie drew in her breath sharply.

"Something that you don't fully understand," he said meaningfully. "You're in love with me—even though you're crazy to be. And you won't admit it to yourself because I'm the last man on earth you ought to love."

Desperately, she tried to pull away from his embrace. But he only drew her closer, holding her gently and tilting back her head so he could see her eyes. She could no longer avoid his gaze. And then, suddenly, she wanted his kisses, his embrace. She felt herself slowly giving in.

"Now I know why you wanted to be alone with me tonight—and why you looked so sad just now when I said you'd never see me again after tomorrow. You love me, Ramona. And I love you, even though you're just as wrong for me as I am for you!"

"Please, let me go," she begged. "You're wrong about me. I swear you're wrong. You see, the truth—"

Astonished at herself, she stopped. If she let herself, she might betray Ramona. Oh, why was it such a struggle for her to keep the truth from this man!

But even if she'd wanted to, Natalie would have found it impossible to speak. Ortega was kissing her cheek, the sensuous touch of his lips erasing all other thoughts, all other worries. She felt herself being carried away on the sweet night air perfumed with oleander, and she only half heard the music of the distant cafés, dulled by the sound of the lapping water. She savored the moment, knowing it would soon be over. Forever.

She tried to withdraw from Ortega's embrace but he held her more closely. Headlights, growing stronger in the dusk, swept by, bathing them in light and then leaving them once again in darkness, locked in one another's arms.

Abruptly, without warning, Ortega let her go. He dug into his pocket for a cigarette and lit it, inhaling deeply. His next words deeply shocked her.

"So, you despise me, do you? Why didn't you call for help? You're a fool if you mistake this for anything more than a passing physical passion. I'm not made of stone and you're a beautiful woman. But don't get the idea that I'm the sort of man to hang around making love to the daughter of a millionaire just to lay my hands on his money!"

Suddenly Natalie lost all control. "Don't flatter yourself, Mr. Ortega! I'd rather die than—"

"Than what?"

But Ortega couldn't hear Natalie's muffled reply as she pushed open the door of the car. Before he could stop her, she ran wildly toward the road.

"Ramona!"

But he was too late. Natalie spotted a horse-drawn cab rounding the curve in the roadway. She raced toward it, waving her arm so that the driver would see her in the twilight. He stopped and looked at her curiously as she stepped into the old fashioned calèche. But he said nothing, for in his day he had seen many young women, tousled and distressed, emerging from the beach. Whistling, he slowly backed his horse.

Natalie, still breathing quickly—whether out of anger or exertion she didn't know—glanced over her shoulder. She could see Ortega standing some distance from the cab, his hands in this pockets, watching her leave with a nonchalant air that infuriated her.

"Don't forget our meeting tomorrow evening at nine!" he called out. "We've got some business to settle."

There was no trace in his voice of the passionate man who'd embraced her only a few moments before. Natalie half wondered if it had all been a dream—or a nightmare.

But as the cab rolled on through the darkness toward the glittering lights of Monte Carlo, she knew it was no dream. With a shudder, she realized how close she'd come to betraying Ramona's secret. Out of love for a scoundrel and a blackmailer.

Chapter 10

The following morning Natalie, tired after an almost sleepless night, went up to see if Ramona had heard from Eduardo yet. She took great pains to seem noncommital about her evening with Jack, not wanting to discuss the awful outcome of her date.

"I came home early because I had a headache," she said dispiritedly.

"Yes," Natalie lied. "I'm just nervous about tonight."

"In fact, you don't look very well. Do you feel all right?"

"Yes." Natalie lied. "I'm just nervous about tonight."

From the uncomfortable look on Ramona's face, Natalie was sure that she hadn't yet heard from her brother. Suspicions flooded her. Maybe Ramona had never even tried to reach Eduardo? Maybe she had become a pawn in a dangerous game only Ramona knew? But that was silly, Natalie scolded herself. Ramona stood to lose a good deal if all this wasn't sorted out—and soon.

"Any word from Eduardo?" Natalie inquired.

"You can relax, Natalie. The money will be here quite soon, I'm sure."

"What do you mean? It has to be here *tonight*!"

Suddenly Natalie was furious. Ramona Martinez had to be made aware that Natalie Davis could stand up for herself. She simply wasn't going to be taken advantage of.

"I promise you, Ramona, if I don't have that money by tonight, I'm not going to that little rendezvous with Marco Ortega. In fact, I'll be on the train back to Paris!"

Ramona winced. She walked over to a small chest by the window and picked up a postcard that had been lying on top of it. Nervously she handed the postcard to Natalie.

"It's from Eduardo," Ramona explained. "He obviously didn't get my telegram. He's flying back to our home in Madrid. I've already sent a cable there telling him that I need the money urgently. I expect it tomorrow or the next day at the latest. The postcard is dated two days ago from Paris, of all places. I'm not sure when he'll arrive but it's bound to be soon. If I haven't heard in a day or so, then I'll have to try tracing him. But that's going to be hard. He's the opposite of me. When he's not hard at work in his practice, he likes to take off by himself."

Ramona's voice had grown very solemn. So, there was a good chance that Ramona would indeed have the money within a day or two, Natalie thought indignantly. But now she was faced with a situation she dreaded. Could she keep Ortega at bay?

"Don't worry," Ramona said hastily, eyeing Natalie in alarm. "I'm almost certain Ortega will go along with it. Surely, if you show him the postcard tonight, he'll agree to wait a couple of more days. After all, he's waited this long."

"Why on earth didn't you tell me this sooner?" Natalie demanded. "Don't you know Ortega means serious business? Oh, never mind! We need to concentrate on how to hold him off. He'll like this as much as I do, I'm sure!" she finished.

"Oh, Natalie! You know how grateful I am for what you're doing for me. And I'm so sorry that you have to go through yet another evening with that man! I'll make it up to you somehow; I promise I will." Ramona's eyes begged forgiveness.

Natalie was silent. How could she explain to Ramona what her feelings were for a man that Ramona had never met—a man who was blackmailing her?

NATALIE WAS JUST FINISHING the last of her mending for the day when the linen-room telephone rang. She picked it up, hoping it wasn't another demand for a torn hem to be sewn before the evening.

"Natalie? Is that you?" Ramona asked breathlessly. "Come up right away. Ortega just called!"

Natalie raced down the hall to the elevator and then along the corridor to Ramona's room. She was waiting at the door for her.

"Ortega just phoned," she said in an excited voice. "He asked to speak to you. I didn't want him to know I wasn't you, so I pretended to be the chambermaid. He left a message for you to call him. Here's the number."

"I wonder what he wants?" Natalie said anxiously. All sorts of unpleasant possibilities crossed her mind and she moved quickly to the phone. "Well, I'd rather know the worst than stand here worrying."

Ramona was visibly upset. "Please, Natalie, hurry! Oh, I hope he isn't going to make matters more difficult!"

Ignoring her, Natalie dialed the number Ramona had given her. Ortega seemed quite calm, though, when he spoke.

"I just wanted to tell you to be sure to dress a little formally tonight, Ramona," he said. He had answered the phone on the first ring and Natalie knew that wherever he was he must have been waiting for her call. "I've booked a table at the Sporting. They're having a special gala evening and I thought you might enjoy it."

But all Natalie could think of were the dangers such an evening would hold for her. The people, many of whom no doubt knew the real Ramona, the sophisticated behavior that the jet set indulged in, might somehow trip her up, reveal her to be an imposter. And there was already going to be trouble enough when she had to tell about the money! No, she didn't like it.

But Ortega, as usual, wouldn't take no for an answer.

"I'm sorry, Ramona. I've made the reservations and that's where we're going. I'm not your friend Jack and I'm not going to bow to your every whim and fancy. I feel like celebrating and I want you to look your best. After all, I do have something to celebrate. So do you, don't forget. This is the last time you'll ever have to see me. And after what happened last night, I thought you'd appreciate my thoughtfulness in choosing such a public place. There'll be no repetition, I can assure you," he ended coolly.

Natalie knew she was defeated.

"Very well, you've convinced me," she said, as gracefully as she could. "The Sporting at nine."

With a short laugh Ortega hung up.

"Well, if that's all he wanted, we had nothing to worry about," Ramona said airily when Natalie had repeated the conversation. "A gala at the Sporting sounds like fun. You'll have a lovely time. I wish I could go."

Natalie glared at her. Ramona smiled sheepishly.

"I'm sorry. It's not that I'm unaware of the risk you're taking on my behalf, Natalie. It's just that, stuck up here day after day, it's hard for me to remember sometimes that . . . well, with your doing all the work, I sometimes forget that anything's the matter."

Natalie understood all right. Ramona, sheltered by all her money, had never got an opportunity to really taste life. Maybe being "poor" and having to make your own way wasn't such a bad thing, she mused.

"Let's decide what you're going to wear," Ramona said, obviously happy to change the subject.

Together they went through Ramona's enormous collection and chose a full-length golden cream dress with a tight bodice and long flowing skirt. With its delicate off-the-shoulder sleeves and fashionably uneven skirt, Ramona thought it made Natalie look like some latter-day Juliet. And, with a mink stole of the softest, most delicate mole color and her hair brushed and flowing full-length behind her, Natalie felt more than able to take on everyone and anyone. Even Marco Ortega.

"Perfect," Ramona said admiringly. "But you need some jewelry. Take these pearls. They're almost priceless, rare Spanish pearls that my grandmother gave me. She said that they would make a plain woman beautiful and a beautiful woman unforgettable. With your tan, they'll look marvelous."

"I thought most of your jewelry was in hock," Natalie said suspiciously.

"Most of it is," Ramona said. "But what's the good of having lovely things if you can't wear them? Besides, even I have sufficient honor not to barter with family heirlooms."

Natalie was about to protest but as Ramona slipped the cool pearl choker around her neck, then the triple strands of the bracelet over her wrist, she stopped. She watched in the mirror as Ramona fastened them and put the last touches to her hair. Taking risks, she thought, did have its compensations, however temporary.

AN ELEGANT, PERFUMED Natalie floated past the doorman at the Sporting and an equally elegant, well-groomed Marco greeted her. As he led her to the table, she could feel the eyes of the crowd follow them.

To Natalie it all seemed like a dream, a dream that might have become a reality if Marco had been a man she could have loved openly. Tonight, she thought, he looked extremely handsome. His eyes were shining and he looked happy as he pulled back a chair for her with a flourish.

"How beautiful you are tonight," he said. He reached for her gloved hand across the table. "I never quite realized how lovely you are until now."

Natalie tried to close her ears to that voice, its sound and its effect on her. The real reason for her date with Ortega was not pleasure, and the lovely feeling of anticipation that she'd felt for a few precious minutes died.

Natalie stole a look at Ortega as he carefully examined the menu the waiter had brought him.

He glanced at her and smiled.

"Before we begin this evening, I want to get one thing straight. This is probably going to be our last night together. Can't we pretend that—just for tonight—we're not enemies?"

When Natalie made no attempt to interrupt him, Ortega continued, "You're a very lovely woman, Ramona, and I find you irresistible. You find me attractive as well, although you've never actually said so. One can sense these things." He looked at her for confirmation, but Natalie kept her eyes lowered, afraid that one glance would betray the torrent of her emotions.

"Surely these are the perfect ingredients for a romantic evening under the stars? I'm asking you to forget everything else that separates us, Ramona; just let yourself be in love with me, for an hour or two. Can you do that?" he finished gently, pouring her a glass of champagne.

Natalie, still unwilling to speak, made a gesture of protest but Marco chose to ignore it. "Let's agree then, that we'll make the evening strictly a social one until midnight. After the fireworks, we'll talk business. Agreed? Ah, then, I'll take your silence to mean yes."

As they chatted about what to order and Marco pointed out his favorite dishes and how they were prepared, Natalie struggled to remember that it would soon be over. They seemed so suited to one another. As long as she could forget who, and what, he was, she could so easily imagine that this was not the end, but the beginning. . . .

Marco attended to her every whim, and spoke with such charm and knowledge on what seemed to be dozens of subjects that, once again, she wondered about his background. Ortega was decidedly a man of wealth and education. But why then had he become a blackmailer?

Perhaps he was the wayward son of a wealthy Spanish family, for hadn't he told her as much? But, Natalie reminded herself, she had long ago chosen not to believe anything a blackmailer—especially one with eyes like Ortega's—claimed.

Ortega was drawing her attention to several celebrities who had just entered the club and he smiled as he saw the faraway look in her eyes. The club was crowded now, for most of Monte Carlo's celebrated visitors dined late at the fashionable restaurant. They all came, Marco explained, to watch the floor show, then to move out to the terrace for the famous display of fireworks.

Natalie was quite amazed at the variety of people she saw. There were the tourists of course, easily recognizable by their slightly bewildered air, but Natalie could see some very famous people as well, all of them elaborately dressed. The women wore an array of jewels that made Natalie, who adored jewelry, secretly sigh in admiration and envy; diamonds, sapphires, rubies and emeralds, all in incredibly varying settings, were everywhere. Even the most simply dressed women wore something that Natalie would have been proud to own.

Suddenly lights flooded the stage and the drums began to beat. The noisy crowd was silent as it turned its attention to the stage. Natalie was not disappointed. There were performances by some of her favorite dancers, as well as lots of popular American jazz that went down particularly well with the audience, who applauded wildly for more.

Ortega, moving his chair closer to hers in order to get a better view of the stage, took Natalie's hand and in a low voice explained that because it was off-season for so many performers, Monte Carlo was able to feature world-class

artists here each summer. He reminded her that at one time
Monaco had been the centre of much avant-garde dance.
He spoke enthusiastically and knowledgeably of the
famous Ballets Russes of Monte Carlo, and its even more
famous impresario Sergei Diaghilev, and of how the great
Russian dancer Vaslav Nijinsky had once sent audiences
not unlike this one into raptures during just such a
Mediterranean summer evening.

As the wine gradually took effect, Natalie felt the music
from the stage recede into the distance. She was really
listening to the music of the sea—and imagining how it
bathed the shore, not just here in southern France but in
distant islands, even other continents. As she sat in what
seemed to her, in her almost trancelike state, to be a perfumed garden, for a moment that was too brief she felt that
she was in paradise.

"You must know that I love you," murmured a voice in
her ear. And suddenly Natalie's worst fears burst over her
head as, in a few minutes, the fireworks would burst in the
soft night sky above her. How could she keep resisting this
man if he made it even harder by claiming to love her?
Swiftly she turned around, looking eagerly for some way
to escape. But Ortega, as if he'd guessed her intent, laid his
hand on her arm.

"Don't be silly. Look, the fireworks are about to begin."

Although Natalie had known this display would out-
class anything she had seen as a child, she wasn't prepared
for the way in which the simple sparklers and Roman
candles had been transformed into what seemed to her,
light-headed with wine and love, to be a supreme art form.

Within seconds it was as if all the jewels that the women
were wearing that night had been tossed high into the sky,

only to burst into a thousand fragments and fall back down to earth in a shower of colors that made the white villas and palm trees along the seashore glow in their reflected light.

As they sat silently watching the firewords through the glassed–in walls, Natalie could feel Marco's shoulders touching her and she was sure that he must be able to hear the beating of her heart. But he seemed calm and said nothing.

Then, as the last of the fireworks died, he turned to her and, for the first time that evening, offered her a cigarette. He smoked for a moment, watching her with steady eyes.

"It's time to talk business," he said finally and with what seemed to Natalie to be reluctance. "Where's the money?"

Without a word Natalie handed him Eduardo's postcard. She could see that he, too, was having a little difficulty returning to the business at hand. He studied the card for some time, then he eyed her suspiciously and his features hardened.

"How soon do you think the money will get here?"

So, he was willing to accept the delay! Natalie took a deep breath, knowing that the worst was over. And now, if she could convince him to give up these meetings and to wait patiently for the money, she wouldn't have to see him again. It would be over, she thought sadly.

"Perhaps by tomorrow. Definitely by the day after," she answered. "It's only forty-eight hours at the most."

"I suppose I can wait a little while longer."

Relieved, Natalie smiled at him. Suddenly he reached across the table and once again took her hand in his.

"Please believe me, Ramona: if I could, I would forget about the money."

Too surprised to speak, Natalie was distracted by the arrival of someone at their table. She looked up. A waiter coughed apologetically, uncomfortably aware that he had interrupted an intimate moment.

"I beg your pardon, sir. But there is an urgent phone call for you."

"Well, can't you bring the phone to our table?" Ortega looked at him impatiently.

"I'm afraid not, sir. Could you please come with me and I'll show you where you can take the call in private."

"I'll be as quick as I can." It was obvious to Natalie that Ortega wasn't expecting this call. He even seemed vaguely alarmed. "Will you be all right?"

She nodded. Here was the chance she'd been waiting for. While Ortega was gone, she would write him a note, explaining that he could call her tomorrow at the hotel to find out if the money had arrived and asking him, if he had any feelings for her at all, not to demand that she see him again.

But as she searched in her purse for a pen and paper, she began to have second thoughts. Might she not be ruining everything? If she ran away now, Ortega might refuse to wait the extra few days. Oh, it was impossible to tell, but dare she risk it? So much counted on this. On the other hand, could she trust herself to spend any more time with him?

A moment later a man walked up to her table and sat down in Ortega's place.

"I beg your pardon, *monsieur*, but there must be some mistake," Natalie said in surprise. "Someone else is sitting there. I mean, he'll be returning shortly."

"If I were you, Miss Martinez, I wouldn't try to make any sudden moves."

As Natalie heard the words, she knew that she had been tricked. Ortega had led her to believe that he was willing to accept the delay when in fact he had no intention of doing so. And what was even more despicable, he had left the table on the pretext of answering some phone call so that someone else could carry out his dirty business.

"I suggest that you don't try to attract attention, Miss Martinez," the dark, wizened little man said quietly. "It will only go worse for you if you do. Although it is out of sight, I have a gun and I will be happy to use it if necessary. On you. Or on anyone else here." He indicated the occupants of the club with a movement of his head.

"What do you want?" Natalie asked, knowing the answer.

"You," came the toneless reply. "In a few minutes, after I've had a glass of wine and you've treated me as if I were a long-lost friend, we're going to get up and leave. Together. As if it were the most natural thing in the world."

Natalie thought the next few minutes would never pass.

"At least tell me your name, if we're going to be such famous friends," she pleaded.

"Manuel."

But she couldn't speak. She listened dully as he mouthed a few platitudes for the benefit of the guests at the next table.

It was obvious that Manuel was as eager to leave as Natalie was. Throwing a few bills on the table, he helped her on with her stole, put his arm through hers and escorted her out of the crowded restaurant.

Natalie felt a surge of physical revulsion flow through her as Manuel touched her and it was all she could do not to draw back. But she could also feel the bulge of a gun under his jacket and she knew that she would be stupid to make any unexpected moves.

As far as she could tell, no one had noticed their exit. Or if they had, no one had seen anything unusual in it. She supposed unhappily that it was common enough in the social circles that frequented the Sporting for a woman to come with one man and leave with another.

There was a car waiting for them outside the club.

"Get in the back seat," Manual ordered.

"Where are you taking me? Where's Ortega?" Natalie cried, as someone inside the car pushed open the back door. Manuel, not so well behaved as he had been in the restaurant, shoved her toward it.

"I don't know what you're talking about," he said gruffly. "Get in the back seat," Manuel ordered.

Frightened, Natalie did as she was told. Apart from herself, Manuel and the driver, there was no one else in the car. It smelled heavily of cigarette smoke.

"Where are you taking me? Please, let me explain to Marco. There's been a mistake." Panic filled her. She was being kidnapped!

Natalie turned to Manuel, who was ignoring her and looking sullenly out the window. "You've got to understand!" she cried desperately.

Suddenly she saw a hand lash out. There was a sharp pain across her face, then blackness. . . .

Chapter 11

Natalie felt terribly tired. With a sigh she turned over, unwilling to get up and face another day of ironing in the overheated linen room. Her head hurt and she ached all over. Vaguely she tried to remember what it was she had been doing that would have caused her to feel so sore.

Her eyes flew open and a sick fear flooded her. She wasn't in the Hotel de Paris. She couldn't be. There had been men . . . guns. Unable to focus clearly, she shut her eyes, trying to remember.

"You'd better have a drink," a voice recommended.

Startled, Natalie opened her eyes once more. A man was standing beside her. He was very tall and dark and held a glass in one hand. Leaning down beside her, he lifted her up to a half-sitting position so that she could drink easily.

"Thank you," she murmured as she gave him back the glass.

Her eyes were beginning to clear and in spite of feeling sick she tried to look around. She was in a tiny room; aging wallpaper hung in shreds from the walls and a window patched with pieces of cardboard barely allowed light to shine through. She had no idea what time it was, although it was obviously day.

"You've been out a long time. Manuel must have really belted you. I told them to go easy, but they don't listen to me," the man said, almost as if he were apologizing.

"Where am I?" Natalie moaned. Now that she was coming to, she realized that she must have been unconscious for several hours. She touched her face gently. Her cheek was swollen.

"It's better that you don't know. I hope you won't be here for very long and then you can just forget this whole thing."

Hearing the sympathy in the man's voice, Natalie knew instinctively that she had an ally. Slowly she struggled to sit up fully, fighting back the waves of nausea. A shock of recognition ran through her as she stared at the man.

"Fernando!"

He seemed surprised but said nothing. He seemed not to remember her and Natalie felt her heart sink.

"Don't you remember me? We met at the harbor in Monte Carlo, one evening about a month ago. You offered me a glass of absinthe and we looked at the boats together," she said in an agony of hope.

Fernando looked at her more closely, hesitating. Natalie, unable to understand why he hadn't recognized her immediately, suddenly remembered her appearance. She was still in her evening dress, although it was now creased and torn. And someone must have covered her with the mink stole. No doubt she looked very different from the simply dressed girl he had briefly talked with in the moonlight a few weeks earlier. She couldn't remember if she'd even mentioned her name. She thought she might have told him to ask for the linen maid if he ever came to the hotel looking for her.

But before Fernando could respond, the door to the tiny room flew open. Two men walked in. One of them Natalie instantly recognized as Manuel. The other one, a huge man dressed in dark trousers and a black sweater with a beret pulled down almost over his eyes, was smoking a cigar.

"I see that Señorita Martinez is awake," he said in a voice that made it clear to Natalie that he didn't give a damn one way or the other.

Natalie's instincts told her that these men—with the possible exception of Fernando, and she couldn't be certain of him, either—were the sort to mistreat her even more if she gave them the impression she was frightened. She straightened up as much as she could on the old narrow cot and, looking up at the man in the beret, said in an offended voice, "Why have you brought me here? I insist on seeing Mr. Ortega. He's making a very foolish mistake and it's going to get him into a lot of trouble."

"That's the same guy she was talking about last night," Manuel said to the man in the beret. "I don't know who she thinks he is."

Natalie watched as the big man came up to her. He didn't say anything but the look in his eyes alarmed her. The smell of his cigar, quickly filling the small, poorly ventilated room, made her feel worse.

"Who is this man, Ortega?" he demanded.

Terror-struck, Natalie stared up at him. Until now she had managed to keep her fear at bay, but if this man wasn't lying and if they really didn't have any connection with Ortega, then who were they?

"Why, *señor*, Mr. Ortega has been blackmailing me. I

was with him yesterday at the Sporting when your man—"
Natalie indicated Manuel, who was standing at the far end
of the room with a hostile expression on his face. It was
clear that he had taken a real dislike to her. "When your
man," she repeated, "insisted I come with him. I naturally
assumed, since I had just told Mr. Ortega that I wouldn't
be able to give him any money for a day or so, that he had
sent Manuel to . . . to kidnap me and keep me until my
brother paid him."

Natalie paused. If these people were in league with
Ortega but had been given instructions to deny it, she felt
it was a good idea to keep on pretending she was Ramona.
If, on the other hand, they had nothing to do with Ortega,
wasn't she just complicating things by continuing to talk as
though she were, in fact, the Spanish heiress? Her panic
was growing. She had never felt so alone, so confused and
frightened in her life.

The man with the cigar looked shrewdly at Natalie.
Without being told, Natalie knew now that these people
had nothing to do with Ortega.

"Señorita Martinez," he began slowly, "I do not know
this man Ortega. I have never met him. We are holding
you for ransom until your father agrees to give in to our
demands. For your sake, you'd better hope that he gives us
what we want—and quickly. Personally, my dear little
Spanish princess, it would give me great pleasure to treat a
woman like you exactly as you deserve to be treated. . . ."

At first Natalie was stunned. How could she believe
what he had just told her? Eyes wide, she watched as he
came closer and jerked her chin up between his fingers.
She tried to draw back but he held her there, forcing her to
raise her eyes to his. Suddenly she found her voice.

"I'm *not* Ramona Martinez," she insisted. "You've got the wrong person. Oh, please listen to me! Señor Martinez will never agree to your demands because I'm *not* his daughter! It won't matter to him what you do with me."

The man with the cigar, obviously assuming that she was hysterical, shrugged his shoulders. He seemed about to leave and Natalie, sensing that she must do something dramatic to force their attention, rolled off the narrow bed with a cry. As she had hoped, he was enough of a gentleman to lean down to help her up. As he did so, she looked deeply into his eyes. "Please," she whispered. "I don't know who you are, but I'm not Ramona Martinez! Can't you at least listen to my story?"

Fernando stepped in.

"Paulo, let's hear her out. It won't hurt and something tells me that we should."

Natalie gave Fernando a grateful smile. He evidently carried some weight with the older man for Paulo grunted his agreement.

"All right. I will listen. But it will take a lot to convince me."

Natalie hardly knew where to begin. She was trembling and Fernando, sensing her fear, said gently, "It's all right. We're listening now. Tell us what you want us to know."

As best as she could, Natalie explained what had happened. At first, she saw a look of disbelief cross Paulo's face and she was sure only Fernando's restraining hand on his shoulder kept him from leaving. But as she continued, she could tell from the expression on their faces that they were beginning to take her more seriously. Exhausted, she finished with a final plea.

"I swear to you, I am not Ramona Martinez. Don't you

agree that my story is just too fantastic to be made up? Can't you see that I'm not the person you think I am?"

Manuel, who had been listening in scorn to everything Natalie had said, now began to rummage in an old dirty knapsack that someone had thrown in one corner of the room. With a sudden cry of triumph, he pulled from it a piece of newspaper and handed it to Paulo with a sneer.

"You can't tell me that this—and her—aren't the same person."

"What is it?" Natalie cried, knowing all too well.

Without a word Paulo handed her a photograph. It was a head-and-shoulders shot of Ramona Martinez. Somehow Natalie had never realized how uncannily alike she and Ramona looked. But now she had to admit that anyone—especially these criminals—who might compare her with this photograph of the real Ramona Martinez would find it hard to believe they were not one and the same. With tears in her eyes, no longer caring who saw them, she looked first at Paulo, then at Fernando. Even to her own ears, her voice sounded desperate and defeated at the same time.

"I know that we look alike," she began. "Otherwise the deception couldn't have worked. But I swear to you that I *am* Natalie Davis!"

"It's a lie," Manuel warned. "You're both fools if you listen to her."

Annoyed, Paulo turned on him. "Shut up. Tell me what you think when I ask you."

Paulo stared hard at Natalie. "We've already communicated with Señor Martinez's headquarters in Madrid. Other members of our organization should be in touch with us shortly to let us know if he's accepted our terms. If what you have told us is true, we'll know soon enough.

In the meantime," Paulo turned to Fernando, "get the *señorita* something to eat. And see if you can find some clothes to fit her. I don't want her dressed like this in case we have to get out of here quickly. She's too conspicuous."

As Paulo left the room followed by Manuel, Natalie couldn't help feeling a rush of hope. After all, he had called her '*señorita*,' and not 'Señorita Martinez.' Was it possible that he believed her after all?

Fernando told her to rest while he went to get food and clothing. Natalie lay back on the cot, her thoughts returning to Ortega. So, he hadn't betrayed her. Somehow, by some bizarre coincidence, these people had been planning to kidnap Ramona and had mistaken *her* for the heiress. It was understandable, of course. Ramona Martinez was often at the Sporting and the photograph would be enough to convince anyone that she herself was Ramona. But now she really was trapped. And truly alone. Ortega had probably disappeared, unwilling to wait for his money. In spite of everything, though, she couldn't help rejoicing in the knowledge that he hadn't betrayed her.

Suddenly Natalie sobbed into the pillow, hoping it would muffle her cries. What did it matter now? It was her own fault, she knew, and that was what hurt most of all. She had been stupid to take such risks. Stupid to forget that a woman like Ramona Martinez could face danger from a number of directions. Intoxicated by the romance and excitement of wealth, she had offered to take Ramona's place, as much because she wanted the adventure as because she felt sorry for Ramona. And then, when she had met Ortega, she had thrown caution to the winds.

Briefly, between sobs, Natalie wondered about Jack. Would he know about her disappearance? Would he try to help find her? How bitterly she now regretted not having taken him into her confidence. Natalie tried to imagine what was happening at the hotel. The management, she was sure, would be furious to discover that she had become mixed up in Ramona's affairs. When—Natalie didn't allow herself to use the word 'if'—she got out of this mess, she knew she would no longer have a summer job at the hotel. And Ramona . . . was she terribly upset, or just relieved that it had been Natalie and not her? Would her father be able to help?

The door opened and closed softly. Hurriedly Natalie sat up and tried to wipe her eyes without letting Fernando, who had just returned, see her. He was tactful enough to ignore the very obvious signs that she had been crying and said gently, "I've brought you some coffee and bread. I'm afraid that's all we have. We're not exactly living in the lap of luxury. And these are some clothes for you to put on."

He held out a pair of khaki-colored trousers and a cotton shirt, setting them and a large pair of scissors on the floor beside him.

"One of the girls, Gabriella, will get you some boots. And cut your hair."

"What?"

"I'm sorry. Paulo's orders. We're going to have to leave here very soon and we have to do everything we can to make sure that if we're stopped by police, you don't look like Ramona Martinez. The fastest way is to cut your hair and dress you in these. I'm sorry," he repeated. Judging from the look in his eyes, Natalie could tell that he meant it.

"Fernando," she said quietly as he handed her the coffee, "how did you get involved in all this? You don't seem like a terrorist to me." And as Natalie said the word, she realized that these people *were* terrorists and that she had known it ever since she had regained consciousness. In a flash she remembered her proud words to Ramona about wanting to be a diplomat and not being frightened of terrorists. Little did she know then how soon she would have an opportunity to test her opinion! Fate—Ramona's explanation—had stepped in to teach her a lesson, it seemed.

"That's what you are, isn't it?"

"It's what other people call us," he admitted.

"Why?" Natalie knew now that it wasn't any use to make him remember the time they'd shared at the harbor. She was sure that he did remember. But she was equally sure that he would never admit it, not now.

"We're not terrorists, Ramona. We're political revolutionaries, dedicated to the overthrow of governments who repress people. We sometimes kidnap people in order to make money. We have to."

"And you believe you have no other choice, no other resources?" Natalie asked softly. She had to find out more about Fernando. He was her only ally and if Señor Martinez refused to help, this man would be her only refuge.

"I'm not uneducated, Ramona. I've studied at universities in England. We are not thugs, you know. We are serious revolutionaries deeply devoted to our struggle."

"And are you as deeply devoted as Manuel?" she asked, scarcely able to believe her boldness. One wrong move and this man could treat her as roughly as he liked. The others, from what she had seen of them, certainly weren't going to come to her protection.

But somehow her instincts told her Fernando disapproved of some of their tactics. And she had to know if her instincts were right.

Fernando looked at her strangely and was about to say

something when the door opened again and a woman entered, carrying a pair of well-worn brown boots.

"Oh, Gabriella." Fernando was obviously relieved to see her. "This is Ramona Martinez. Will you watch out for her while she changes? Then cut her hair with these." Fernando held out the scissors.

"We should know very soon what your father's reaction to our message is," he said, preparing to leave.

"Fernando, he's *not* my father!" Natalie insisted, but he ignored her and left the room.

Natalie looked at Gabriella with curiosity. In spite of her fear, she was intrigued. She had never seen a woman revolutionary before, not in person.

"Put them on," Gabriella motioned to the clothes Fernando had brought in. "We're in a hurry."

Slowly Natalie got off the bed and began to undress. Gabriella was looking at her evening dress closely as Natalie slipped it off. As she pulled on the trousers and shirt, her hands went to the pearl choker around her neck.

"I'll take that," Gabriella said.

Natalie hesitated. It wasn't that she cared for the pearls. After all, they were Ramona's and any sentimental value they had would be for her. But somehow she was reluctant to part with them. They were her last tangible link with the world from which she had been taken and to which she desperately wanted to return.

"Here, put on these boots," Gabriella ordered. "They're mine and they should fit you. And give me those pearls."

Natalie undid the choker and the bracelet, then silently handed them to Gabriella, who shoved them into the pocket of her trousers.

"All right. Now sit on the edge of the bed. I'm going to cut your hair."

"No!" Suddenly it was just too much. Jumping up from the bed, Natalie ran to the other end of the tiny room.

"You're not going to touch me!" she shouted.

"That's what you think!" Gabriella snapped. "Sit down on the bed, I say!"

The door was suddenly flung open. Paulo, followed by Fernando and a man Natalie hadn't seen before, stormed in. Natalie was sobbing hysterically and Gabriella, the scissors held menacingly in one hand, was glaring at her with a look of pure hatred.

"By the saints, what is going on here?" Paulo thundered.

"She's going to hurt me with those scissors," Natalie cried.

"She's a liar," Gabriella hissed. "What else can you expect from someone like her but lies?"

Paulo grabbed the scissors from Gabriella's hand. "Here, Fernando, help me with this."

And together the two of them cut off inches of Natalie's hair. Holding large strands of it in his hands, Paulo hacked away. It wasn't the pulling of the scissors, although it did hurt, that brought tears to Natalie's eyes, but rather the indignity and the memory of how she had wondered idly whether or not to have her hair cut only a few days earlier. Now someone else had made that decision for her.

"It doesn't look bad," Fernando commented.

Natalie looked at him angrily but dared not say anything. Didn't he realize that she wasn't worried about her hair? It would grow back soon enough. What upset her was her helplessness in the hands of these men, and the unfairness that she, Natalie Davis, should be risking her life for someone else.

"Well, your little trick hasn't worked, Señorita Martinez," Paulo said suddenly. "My friend here, Emile, has spoken with your father. He has agreed to accept our terms."

Natalie didn't know how to react: whether to be overjoyed at the obvious indication that Señor Martinez and Ramona were doing everything they could for her, or whether to wish that they'd told the kidnappers the truth and advised them to free her immediately. But, she reminded herself, she knew nothing of these matters. She could only trust that the Martinezes were doing their best for her.

She stared dully at Paulo. All she saw in his expression was contempt, and suddenly she didn't care anymore. She felt sick—sick with fatigue and hunger, sick with anger at these people for treating her this way. But there was nothing she could do.

Turning to Fernando, Paulo spoke to him rapidly in almost unintelligible Spanish. "You'd better get her ready. We're leaving in a few minutes. I want to travel when it's dark."

"Fernando, where are you taking me?" Natalie cried as soon as the others had left.

"I can't tell you," he said gently. "But I promise that I'll do my best to make sure that you're not hurt."

"Where are we?" Natalie was certain that they weren't in Monte Carlo.

"I'm very sorry, but it's better that you don't know."

Natalie could not check the tears that rolled down her cheeks. She felt so alone, so abandoned. . . . And then Fernando's arms were around her and she felt his reassuring presence.

"Don't worry," he said into her ear. "I'll look after you. Please don't cry."

But Fernando couldn't possibly know, Natalie thought as she fought uselessly to hold back her tears—for his sake now because he seemed genuinely upset by her crying—that the comfort of his arms around her made it impossible not to cry.

THE CAR THEY TRAVELED IN wasn't the same as the one Manuel had used the night before. It was much larger, Natalie thought. But she couldn't be certain. She squirmed uncomfortably, for Paulo had insisted that she be blindfolded. Fernando had protested but Paulo had been adamant.

"Remember who she is," he said angrily, "and what this means to us."

Since then, Fernando had kept his distance from her. It was obvious to Natalie that he didn't fit in with these people. For one thing he looked too healthy. He was in excellent condition from his work as a sailor and he seemed to be a happy person. The others seemed to be constantly quarreling among themselves or competing for Paulo's attention.

Natalie had tried to figure out how many of the terrorists there were but they had carefully blindfolded her before leading her out to the car. She had been taken down a long stairway of crumbling stone to the waiting vehicle and she had no idea of where she was or where she was going.

Yet she was pretty sure there were only four of them:

Paulo, Fernando, Gabriella and herself. And she knew
there were guns because she could feel them at her feet. She
had jumped when Paulo mentioned this and Fernando, still
sensitive to her feelings, had said reassuringly, "Don't
worry, the safety catch is on."

Natalie had been far from reassured. Still, she conveyed
a silent thank-you to Fernando, then turned her attention
to figuring out where they might be taking her.

At first Natalie had no idea whatsoever. But gradually
she began to piece together bits of information, and by
listening very carefully to their cryptic conversation, she
decided that they had to be driving through a large city.
The car's frequent stops— for street lights, she assumed—
and the sound of people helped convince her. And then,
suddenly, it seemed obvious. Marseilles! Of course; it was
large enough to afford them the anonymity they needed,
and close enough to various kinds of transportation in case
they had to separate and get away quickly. For a moment,
Natalie was proud of herself. But where were they taking
her?

She had lost track of time, too. She didn't know whether
it was now the day after her evening with Ortega or even if
more than twenty-four hours had passed. All at once the
memory of that evening, so distant now, and of Ortega's
hand on hers, his voice in her ear, crowded her thoughts.
She would never see him again, and she was filled with a
bittersweet pain.

But the thick material of the scarf that Gabriella had tied
tightly around her head was beginning to hurt her eyes and
make her head ache. There was no time to think of Ortega,
or of anything except her present predicament.

"This is going to be a long trip, Señorita Martinez,"

Paulo abruptly commented. "I suggest that you take the little pill Gabriella has for you. It will make this less difficult to endure."

Desperate for oblivion and no longer caring what risk she was taking Natalie reached out her hand almost eagerly. Gabriella pressed a small capsule into her palm. Natalie swallowed it quickly, praying that its effect would be fast and powerful.

NATALIE MOANED AND PUSHED away the hands that were shaking her. But as they persisted, she felt consciousness returning and stubbornly resisted, unwilling, although she couldn't remember why, to surface into reality.

"Señorita Martinez," a voice that she vaguely recognized was saying repeatedly. "You must wake up! It's almost over. Wake up!"

And then she was awake. Her mouth felt dry and the faces looking at her were indistinct. But, Natalie found herself thinking, whatever they had given her had only been strong, though not dangerous. Her mind felt clear.

"Where are we?" she cried, sitting up suddenly and falling back just as quickly as a wave of dizziness engulfed her.

"Never mind," said Gabriella.

And then Natalie felt her head being grasped. Gabriella was checking the blindfold, but Natalie reacted instinctively, resisting Gabriella's efforts. Someone grabbed her hands and pulled them rudely behind her back, then tied them with a piece of rope. Was it Fernando?

"You'll stay like that until we're rid of you." Paulo's voice was impatient. "Gabriella, change places with Fernando."

Natalie realized that the car had stopped. But where were they? How long had she been drugged? She began to feel that her sense of self was gradually being stripped away, and she trembled as someone slid along the seat, edging closer to her.

It was Fernando. He took her hand in his and whispered, "Hang on. It's almost over. Soon you'll be with your father again."

Natalie was comforted by Fernando's words. She leaned against his shoulder and snuggled close to him, too exhausted with fatigue and fear to think about what might happen to her.

As she drove she sensed that they were now passing through a different country. For one thing the road was steep, with sharp turns and deep dips. But try as she might, her mind was too sluggish to grapple with their whereabouts.

Suddenly the car speeded up. Natalie tensed.

Fernando squeezed her arm, saying, "It's all right. He just doesn't want to be late. We're almost there."

After a few more moments, Natalie could feel the car turn off the main highway and onto a rougher, probably gravel-covered road. Something brushed against the roof of the car; it sounded like the scrape of tree branches to Natalie's ears. Paulo drove very carefully through what she guessed was a narrow, overgrown road. By the time the car drew to a halt, she felt drained, and doubted, if she had to run for it, whether she would have the strength.

Fresh air rushed into the car. Fernando slipped his arm under her shoulder and said encouragingly, "Come on. Your father's waiting for you."

Helped by Fernando, for her hands were still tied behind

her back, Natalie slid out of the car and stood up in the cool air. Fernando's strong arms were supporting her as they walked slowly along what seemed like a narrow path.

To Natalie, unable to see, the quiet seemed ominous. She had no idea where Paulo and Gabriella were and she wondered, suddenly fearful for Fernando, if the others had abandoned him. She was certain, although she couldn't say why, that they suspected him of being less enthusiastic about their cause than they thought he should be. Had they given him the job of turning her over to Señor Martinez in the hope that he would be killed, she wondered in cold fear.

"Fernando," she whispered, "go. There's going to be trouble. I know it."

"Don't be silly," he answered. "Here, be careful. You're going to fall. Hold onto me."

A shout suddenly split the stillness. Natalie started but Fernando grabbed her. And then chaos broke loose. As Fernando pushed her, Natalie felt herself falling, unable to stop herself. The sound of automatic rifle fire filled the air and she screamed.

"Natalie!"

Desperately, she crawled forward, branches pulling and scraping her, trying to move in the direction of the cry.

"Get her before she reaches them!" someone yelled.

"No!" Fernando cried.

A bullet tore through the air and suddenly strong arms were holding her. She felt herself being lifted up and carried away. A voice, familiar and unexpected, was whispering tenderly in her ear.

"Oh, my darling! You're safe now, I promise. And I'll never let you out of my sight again."

Chapter 12

"Natalie, how are you feeling?" someone was asking anxiously.

Warm and comfortable in a deep bed, Natalie murmured and rolled over. Suddenly she was awake, the memory of the past few days jolting her to her senses.

"Where am I?" she demanded, sitting upright.

Ramona was beside her and seeing that she was awake at last, she threw her arms around Natalie.

"Oh, please forgive me!" Ramona pleaded. Then she burst into tears.

Confused, Natalie could only stammer, "But where am I? I remember—"

"Oh, Natalie!" Ramona wailed. "If it hadn't been for me none of this would have happened. You risked your life for me. If anything had happened to you I would have died from guilt!"

Natalie sank back against the pillows. How could she have heard Ortega? Had he carried her here or was it only a dream? She stared at Ramona, who, dressed in a rich crimson silk dress, her hair piled gracefully on her head, now looked a picture of health and vitality—except for the obvious distress in her expression.

"It was so terrible!" Ramona went on. "When you didn't return from the Sporting I was so worried and I didn't know what to do! Fortunately Eduardo arrived and I told him everything. He immediately called my father in New York. By then my father had already been contacted by the kidnappers. He was frantic! Eduardo got to him just in time and explained that I was all right but that you were in great danger. They agreed to meet the demands of the terrorists and arranged for the exchange to take place in Switzerland."

"Are we in Switzerland?" Natalie asked. "What day is it?" She was still trying to get her bearings.

"It's Friday. You've been asleep for almost twenty-four hours!"

Sensing that her friend was still trying to reorient herself, Ramona went on, "Eduardo took an enormous risk, not contacting the police. But we decided to use our own private resources and it worked. Once you were safe, we did tell the police. They are holding the ones whose prisoner you were on their way back to France."

"But I heard gunfire," Natalie said, puzzled.

"Oh, yes, one of our men opened fire. But Eduardo managed to reach you. One of the terrorists was injured, though."

"Fernando!" Suddenly it all came back to her. The ride . . . Fernando's kindness, his hand shoving her forward into Ortega's arms as shots rang out.

"Do you know what happened to him, the terrorist who was shot?" Natalie asked anxiously.

"Why, no." Ramona looked at Natalie oddly. Natalie

could see that she was surprised by the question and considered that her friend must still be suffering from the effects of her ordeal.

"You said that it was Eduardo who found me? Are you sure?" Natalie demanded, recalling Ramona's words. *Had* she only been dreaming, her thoughts a blur from the drugs?

"Why, of course it was Eduardo," Ramona replied. "He was so terribly worried about you. My father tried to persuade him not to, but he insisted. He's just across the hall in my room, and he's eager to see you. Do you feel well enough to get up?"

Suddenly Natalie realized that she did. And that she was very hungry. As if reading her mind, Ramona smiled.

"Why don't I order you some lunch and then we can have coffee with Eduardo in my suite?"

After a large luncheon, a bath and a change of clothes, Natalie found herself feeling like a different person. But she was still unable to put the disconcerting memory of Ortega out of her mind. How could he have rescued her when Ramona claimed her brother had? Unless Ramona was lying?

"You've lost weight," Ramona commented as she looked at her. "But you look very well, considering what you've been through."

Natalie had to admit that Ramona was right. Dressed in a simple navy blue linen dress, with a cashmere sweater thrown casually over her shoulders, she certainly didn't look like someone who, less than twenty-four hours earlier, had been in the hands of terrorists. And, she was relieved to discover, the memories were already becoming more distant.

Over the excellent lunch that she'd consumed with a hearty appetite, Ramona had explained to her that she and Eduardo wanted her to return with them the following day to Madrid. She was invited—almost ordered—to spend the rest of her summer there with them, or in their house in the Canary Islands, if she chose.

"It's the least we can do," Ramona had insisted. "You'll need time to recover your strength. And besides," she added smilingly, "you'll be good company and keep me out of trouble."

The matter settled, Natalie had wanted to know about Marco Ortega.

"What happend to him?" she asked in a tense voice.

Ramona seemed not to notice Natalie's anxiety.

"Who knows?" She shrugged her shoulders. "He must have realized that much bigger fish were involved when he returned to the Sporting and found you had disappeared. We never heard from him."

Thoughtful, Natalie had finished her lunch in silence.

Ramona was obviously eager for Natalie to meet her brother, for as soon as her friend had put down her coffee, she said hopefully, "Are you finished? Let's order more coffee upstairs. Eduardo is waiting."

Although Natalie was amused by Ramona's eagerness, she was happy to comply. She was curious to meet Eduardo Martinez, the man on whom they'd both depended for so much during the last while. She had no idea what to expect, but guessed that since he was a doctor, he was probably a well-organized, efficient man, as kind as Ramona was eccentric.

Ramona went ahead to join Eduardo and order the coffee while Natalie stopped off at her room to tidy her hair.

Soon she was walking the short distance down the thickly carpeted corridor to Ramona's suite. She knocked softly on the door, for she could hear the sound of conversation inside.

"Come in, Natalie," Ramona called.

Ramona was sitting opposite Eduardo, who was facing away from the door and as Natalie entered, she stood up. She was smiling, obviously delighted that her brother and her friend were at last meeting each other.

"Natalie, I'd like you to meet Eduardo."

Eduardo turned in his seat to look at Natalie. Then he stood up and strolled toward her, his hand outstretched.

"I can't tell you how happy I am to make your acquaintance . . . Miss Davis."

Ramona looked with some surprise at Natalie when, after a few moments, it became obvious that her friend was not going to reply to Eduardo's friendly greeting.

"Natalie, this is no time to be shy," she pouted. "How unlike you! Eduardo, don't just stand there! The least you could do is thank my friend for all she's done for me."

Natalie, who had backed away from Eduardo, barely heard her. Nor was she able to hide her burning cheeks from Eduardo's insistent, amused gaze.

"Say something, Natalie, for goodness' sake! What's the matter?" Ramona was beginning to get really impatient now.

"Yes, Natalie, do pull yourself together," Eduardo said smilingly. "Let's at least shake hands."

Natalie stood silently, her arms tightly at her side, unable to move. How could . . . ?

Eduardo turned to his sister. "I believe that I can explain the reason for Miss Davis's silence, Ramona," he went on. "You see, she has mistaken me for Marco Ortega."

"Marco Ortega!" Ramona laughed. "Natalie, you must be crazy!"

"Oh, but she isn't," Eduardo said smoothly. "I'm afraid that Natalie is quite right. I *am* the blackmailer she's been dealing with. There's only one Marco Ortega. Unlike you, Ramona, I was unable to find anyone else to play my part."

Ramona gasped. "You meant that there is no real Marco Ortega? That you . . . you engineered this whole thing just to scare me?"

"Not just to scare you, little one," her brother said gently. "I wanted to teach you a lesson that you would never forget as long as you live—and I sincerely hope that I have." Eduardo was perfectly serious now.

Ramona lowered her head and said softly, "I promise that I'll never gamble again, Eduardo. I give you my word before God."

Eduardo looked at her affectionately. "I know that you'll have difficulty keeping that promise, my dear. But I believe that you will succeed and, I assure you, it will get easier. I've been afraid for you," he explained. "You'd embarked on a very dangerous course, Ramona, and I was afraid that I wouldn't be able to stop you before it was too late and you'd become permanently addicted."

"I know, Eduardo. I was just kidding myself that the pleasure was worth the risks. But I was so good at it—at least at first—and everybody I knew gambled."

Eduardo turned to Natalie, hoping that the conversation with his sister had given her time to compose herself. He smiled, his eyes warm with tenderness.

"Do come and sit down, Natalie," he invited. "I still don't think that you should overexert yourself."

Ramona supported him.

"Oh, yes, Natalie. Come and sit down beside me. Let's hear how he dreamed up this crazy scheme of his that had us both so frightened."

Still speechless, for her initial shock was rapidly turning to anger, Natalie took a seat beside Ramona. Eduardo sat opposite them and poured out the coffee. Natalie forced herself to at least listen to Eduardo's account of the entire affair, willing herself to maintain her self-control until she had heard the entire story.

"It's really very simple," Eduardo began. "It was Carlos Vilar who first alerted me to what was going on. After Ramona and my father left for Monte Carlo, I stayed on in Madrid for a few days, trying to decide how to spend my vacation. The trip I'd planned to Japan had fallen through. They'd changed the convention program by calling in some speakers I wasn't too interested in, and I had time to play with. But I wasn't sure how to use it."

"I thought that maybe you'd decided to travel to Japan, stopping off at various places on the way," Ramona put in. "I know how you like to travel by motorcycle."

"It would have been a long trip by bike," Eduardo laughed, "though I suppose possible for part of such a journey. Anyway, I was trying to make up my mind when Carlos phoned me from Monte Carlo. He told me that you were making a bit of a fool of yourself, Ramona. After father had left for the United States, you continued gambling, and in order to pay your debts, you had even resorted to borrowing from him. And it was clear that you had no real intention of stopping."

Ramona blushed and toyed with the hem of her skirt. It was obvious to Natalie that Ramona was deeply influenced by her brother's opinion. She certainly didn't seem to enjoy his disapproval.

"Well, Vilar's phone call convinced me that I should go straight to Monte Carlo to see what I could do about the situation," Eduardo continued. "Evidently the lectures that father gave you, and even the arrangement he made with the hotel management and the banks, were not sufficient. More drastic measures were required. Since father still wasn't very well, I didn't want to worry him, and so I decided to handle matters by myself.

"By the time I reached Monte Carlo, Vilar had informed me that things had gone from bad to worse: you had even given him a bad check. That was when I realized that the lecture I was prepared to give you wouldn't be enough. Carlos had begun to get tough with you, too, for he was as concerned about your gambling as I was. Even more because he didn't want to lose you."

Eduardo paused to take a cigarette from his blazer pocket. Natalie instantly recognized the gesture, the familiar hands, tanned and strong. Still she found it hard to associate the brotherly, authoritative Eduardo Martinez with the elegant, moody Ortega.

"He played his part very well, don't you think?" Eduardo smiled mischieviously at his sister.

Ramona sighed. "Carlos hurt me a great deal. I couldn't understand how anyone who claimed to love me could do that. I still don't and I'm not sure Carlos ever cared for me, despite what you say. As for you and your little drama, Eduardo, it wouldn't have lasted very long if I, and not Natalie, had turned up at that first meeting. Just what would you have done if I had?"

Eduardo shrugged. Once again Natalie recognized the gesture and a pang shot through her. But how dared he have done something so outrageous as to blackmail his *sister*? She bit back the angry words, knowing full well how resourceful Ramona could be.

"We had no intention of torturing you for days and days," Eduardo said to Ramona. "I knew what you'd go through just thinking about being blackmailed, about what it would do to your reputation and to father. I thought it would be enough to cure you. And I knew that if it wasn't, then you were truly a lost cause. I imagined that after you'd sweated out that first day and come down to the Yachtman to meet me, you'd have suffered enough. At that point I'd planned to give you the lecture I'd been going to give you in the first place."

"It didn't quite turn out that way." Ramona gave him an odd little smile.

"That's right, it didn't. As for poor Carlos, he's still in Madrid, waiting for a signal from me that everything is all worked out. He knows, of course, that you're safe, Ramona. And he knows about you, Natalie. When the kidnapping occurred, I called him. But we figured that there was little that he could do—" Eduardo looked meaningfully at Ramona "—for the time being. He sent you the postcard, by the way, that was supposed to be from me. I *had* to stay on in Monte Carlo in order to keep playing the role of Marco Ortega. It was vital, if the plan was going to work that you not suspect a thing."

Eduardo glanced at Natalie, who was wondering if everything he was saying was true. When he described his behavior in this way, it was as if everything he had done had been for his sister. Natalie felt humiliated with herself

for even thinking that he found her attractive. Had he kissed
her for Ramona's sake as well? Blushing, she caught him
looking at her and turned away quickly.

"As soon as I realized that you'd found someone to take
your place, I was curious. Natalie didn't seem your usual
choice in friends and I wanted to find out more about her.
So I decided to pretend to fall into your little trap. I kept
on seeing the other Ramona and even introduced her to
Maria."

"Maria!" Ramona echoed. "I didn't know that she was in
Monte Carlo! So that's why she didn't come to see me as
she'd promised."

Eduardo nodded. "Yes, and she confirmed what I
suspected, that Natalie was a new person in your life.
Maria had never seen her before." His eyes lighted on
Natalie.

"By now, I was even more curious. I had nothing to lose
by continuing to play along, since I held the trump card.
And besides, I was curious to see how long you would be
able to hold out."

Unable to stand it any longer, Natalie got quickly to her
feet. She knocked over a coffee cup in her haste but fortunately it was empty and only rocked back and forth
noisily on its saucer. Unperturbed, Eduardo leaned over to
still it with his hand.

"What is it, Natalie?" Ramona asked anxiously.

"I hope you'll forgive me, Ramona," Natalie said, turning to her friend, "but I can't stay here one more minute.
Please understand: I thank you for arranging my freedom,
but I don't belong here and since you no longer need me,
frankly I'd rather be on my way. I want to go back to living a normal life—"

"Natalie!" a stunned Ramona cried. But she was too late. Natalie had turned and run through the door. Ramona gazed at Eduardo, who was staring down at the carpet, his forehead furrowed.

He looked at Ramona with an expression that she didn't understand.

"Go to her, Ramona. Try to convince her to stay."

Ramona, who had fully intended to do what Eduardo suggested, quickly nodded.

Moments later she found Natalie flipping through the pages of a telephone directory.

"Natalie, what are you doing? You can't possibly be thinking of leaving us now."

"I have to, Ramona. I'll manage somehow. I'll ask Jack to lend me the money." Although she'd said this only to convince Ramona that she did know what she was doing, as soon as the words were out of her mouth, Natalie knew that was exactly what she would do.

"I don't understand. I've invited you to come to Madrid with us. You know that you need the rest and you can't possibly be too proud to accept my offer. After all you've done for me, all you've risked for me, even someone as proud as yourself should be able to accept such an offer. Please . . ." Ramona begged.

Natalie, realizing that Ramona deserved an explanation, said quietly, "It has nothing to do with that, Ramona. It's difficult for me to explain, but—"

"Is it because you've found out that Marco Ortega was really my brother? Is that it? But you should be relieved, Natalie. It means that you weren't in any real danger until—"

"Your brother's made a complete fool of me!" Natalie cut in.

"Made a fool of you! How?" Ramona was shocked. "I know it's not very pleasant to discover that someone has been tricking you, and under such circumstances . . . and after everything else that has happened, I can see how it's difficult for you not to react. But, Natalie, " and Ramona's voice became softly pleading, "that's exactly why I want you to stay with me for a while. You're exhausted, and no wonder! Please, think about it. At least wait until tomorrow to make up your mind."

Perhaps Ramona was right, Natalie reasoned, a little calmer now. But no, she had got into this mess in the first place because she'd been so taken in by Ramona. She would leave and put both Ramona and her disgraceful brother, Eduardo, out of her mind once and for all.

Ramona, seeking out every possible way to convince her friend to stay, said earnestly, "I know Eduardo very well. He would never have pretended to blackmail me for so long if he hadn't found you both attractive *and* interesting. My brother is a man of the world and he knows many famous and accomplished women. But he's also easily bored. You must have have made quite a conquest."

Unaware that these words were the final straw for Natalie, Ramona smiled, certain that her friend would reconsider now and stay.

"I don't care whether your brother finds me attractive or not," Natalie said in a low voice. "He and I are from completely different worlds and it's better to keep it that way. And I made a great mistake getting involved with something that was none of my business."

"Natalie, why are you being so stubborn?" Ramona's voice was hurt. "You know how much you mean to me."

Unable to bear the pained look in Ramona's eyes, Natalie hugged her briefly. Suddenly the tears that she had been holding back all morning poured out and she began to sob as if her heart would break. Ramona, assuming this was all part of her friend's reaction to her recent stress, spoke soothingly.

"I understand. And you will accept my invitation, won't you?"

"Ramona, believe me," Natalie sobbed. "I don't want to offend you. It's just that you can't possibly understand. . . ."

"Understand what, Natalie?" Ramona was puzzled.

But before Natalie could say a word, a voice from the doorway interrupted them. It was Eduardo.

"Ramona, I'd like to talk to Natalie alone for a minute. Do you mind waiting for us in the other room?"

Natalie could sense Ramona's hesitation. But it was only momentary. With a curious glance at her brother, Ramona slipped out of the room.

Natalie didn't know what to do. She didn't want Eduardo to see her like this, to know that he had the power to upset her, but it was too late to hide the tears.

Eduardo came up to her and took both her hands in his. Now that they were face to face, Natalie sensed a change in him. He seemed more like the Ortega she had known.

"Natalie, you're not leaving," he said commandingly. "If you go now in a moment of anger, however understandable, you'll be making a terrible mistake. Perhaps the worst mistake of your life. We must talk, my darling. There is so much to say."

At these words, Natalie's anger exploded.

"Don't call me 'darling.' I'm not your 'darling.' You tricked me! I'll never forgive you for that. You took me for . . . for someone who was only out for money, didn't you? And you thought I was —"

Eduardo drew her closer and she struggled against his embrace. She could feel her anger abating and it frightened her. She didn't want to give in to the feelings she had for this man.

"I'll never forgive myself for the things I said to you, Natalie. But you have to understand my position. I had no idea who you were. For all I knew, you were an unscrupulous woman who had somehow managed to take advantage of my sister—who, as you know only too well, is naive and easily influenced. It seemed feasible to me, too, that you might be involved in some sort of blackmail. And, Natalie, my darling, I got carried away with the game I was playing. If what I sensed you felt was genuine or not—"

Before Natalie could utter a word, he was pressing light kisses on her forehead, her eyes.

"I'm so sorry! How could I have distrusted you or your motives, my darling?" he continued. "I had a chance to see your loyalty to Jack, almost from the time we met. No girl whose only interest was money would run around Monte Carlo with a man like Jack. Please, I don't mean to insult your friend. I am trying to tell you that I was reacting against my own instincts. Because, as I sensed my feelings for you were growing stronger, I became concerned. I wanted our evenings together to go on and on. Yet I knew that you weren't who you claimed to be. Neither was I. We were caught in a terrible trap and I didn't know if our feelings were genuine. . . ."

"I felt the same way," Natalie found herself saying shyly. "I never knew what to believe. I couldn't believe—I didn't want to believe—that I was falling in love with a blackmailer!"

Eduardo chuckled. "And I, I didn't want to believe that I was falling in love with an adventuress who, once she knew who I was, was bound to want to marry me. Or worse, blackmail me if she could! I knew how vulnerable love makes one, my darling. But as for thinking of you as completely without scruples," he murmured, lightly kissing her throat, "I would have had to be totally inexperienced to think that of you! That pitiful little kiss . . . ."

Natalie stiffened.

"Pitiful little kiss!" she said in astonishment, drawing back. Eduardo looked at her in amusement.

"Haven't you thought what it must have meant to me? To kiss a man I couldn't trust, let alone respect?" she demanded. "I assure you, 'Mr. Martinez,' that if I had been able to help myself, I would never let myself get within ten feet of you!"

Eduardo's laughter filled the entire room as Natalie, aghast at what she had just said, realized she had confessed everything to Eduardo.

"So, now you know how I felt about you," she said uncertainly. "Let me go now."

"Natalie, look at me." Eduardo's command was gentle and tender. And finally, unable to help herself, she did look at him, her eyes bewildered and full of unshed tears. It was Eduardo who was smiling at her now, piercing the very depths of her being. Ortega the blackmailer was gone. But the same smile, the dark eyes that drew hers like magnets, were still the same. And so were her feelings for this man.

"Listen to me, my darling. I wanted that kiss to be something much more than just a kiss between us. I wanted it to be a solemn vow. The beginning of a new life for both of us, a life that we would spend together. . . .

"When I returned to the Sporting and discovered you were gone, I was shocked. And more desperate than I've ever been in my life." His eyes searched hers, as if to convince her of the truth of his words. But Natalie no longer needed convincing. Eduardo smiled down at her.

"I knew that something terrible had happened," he said, caressing her cheek. "It was for Ramona's sake that I didn't tell her the full story, that I was Ortega. I thought that it was best to go slowly. I wasn't sure what I was getting into. But the hours of waiting, of uncertainty . . . and the feeling I had when I saw you yesterday with the terrorists convinced me that my feelings for you were the feelings of a lifetime. All the misunderstandings mean nothing in the face of that feeling, my darling."

Tears of happiness streaming down her cheeks, Natalie cuddled closer in Eduardo's arms. She felt herself, at last, at home and at peace. Eduardo's voice continued in her ear, "I can tell you now that I love you. With my heart and soul. Just let us be together. I promise you that I will make you happy. Darling Lili . . . ."

THEY WERE TALKING and laughing happily together when Ramona burst in.

"Oh, I've just spoken to Carlos," Ramona announced breathlessly. "He'll be in Geneva this evening. And he's forgiven me for everything! We're going to be married as soon as possible!"

As Natalie and Eduardo rushed to congratulate her, Ramona looked at them shrewdly. A broad and knowing smile swept across her face, and she hugged them both, jumping up and down in her excitement. Eduardo laughed at her.

"Well, tell us when you're planning to have the wedding," he urged. "We'll make it a double one!"

"Oh, I'll phone Papa right away!" Ramona cried. "I'm so glad that you encouraged him to stay out of this affair, Eduardo." Ramona was regarding her brother with open admiration. "This way, he will only know the joy, not our struggles." Ramona winked at Natalie. "He's wanted Eduardo to get married for years. We had begun to despair of his ever settling down."

"And he'll be delighted to know that you're marrying Carlos," Eduardo added. "He's always encouraged your relationship with him, for he hoped he would be a steadying influence on you."

"Oh, he will be." Ramona smiled happily. "And it will be such a big wedding," she said enthusiastically. Natalie laughed. She could see Ramona was already busy making plans.

"We'll invite *everybody*," Ramona said excitedly. "Natalie, you must wire all your friends immediately to—"

"Even Jack?" Eduardo put in. "I understand he may be busy."

"What do you mean?" Natalie asked. "Surely—"

"Well," Eduardo said importantly, "as soon as I knew you were safe and sound, Natalie, I wired him in Monte Carlo. He's gone back to England now, but he said to tell you that he'd met someone special and that while he'll always love you devotedly, he is deserting you for this someone."

Natalie was delighted. Ramona's reaction, however, took her aback.

"A triple wedding?" her friend said dubiously. "Wouldn't that be—"

"Out of the question," Natalie finished.

Eduardo kissed the tip of her nose. "Tonight," he announced, "the four of us are going to have the most superb dinner Geneva can offer, in celebration of this most extraordinary day!"

What readers say about Mystique Books

"Mystique Books are so exciting and fast-moving that it really *is* hard to put them down."
L.R. and M.R.* Pennsburg, Pennsylvania

"Mystique Books let you relax and enjoy your imagination."
W.E.D., West Allis, Wisconsin

"Mystique Books are exciting, romantic, interesting and mysterious. I can hardly put them down."
E.R., Waterford, Wisconsin

*Names available on request.